What the critics are saying...

4 ½ STARS AND TOP PICK! Burton writes with vivid attention to detail, smooth pacing and an exquisite emotional edge. ~ *Reviewed by Robin Taylor Romantic Times Book Club Magazine*

Jaci Burton shows the realism of BDSM, and she does it well with her brand of human emotions, delicacy and a sure hand. Ms. Burton's characters are treated and portrayed as family when written by her hand. That is a key reason that no matter the genre, I always read Jaci Burton. *Bound to Trust* is a great erotic romance that might just surprise a reader. There was more to it than even I thought there was. Let your imagination soar while reading *Bound to Trust*...you might just come to trust in this author for a great and exciting read every time! ~ *Reviewed by Tracey West Road to Romance*

Wow! Jaci Burton has a definite winner in BOUND TO TRUST. Emotions fly off each page, well crafted as only someone as talented as Ms. Burton can write. ~ *Reviewed by Angela Camp Romance Reviews Today*

Ms Burton has again demonstrated her mastery in creating believable conflicts and relationships that draw her readers into her characters' world. ~ *Reviewed by Dawn Brookes*

BOUND OF TRUST
CHAINS OF LOVE

Bound of Trust
An Ellora's Cave Publication, January 2005

Ellora's Cave Publishing, Inc.
1337 Commerce Drive
Stow, Ohio 44224

ISBN #1419951009
Other available formats: ISBN MS Reader (LIT), Adobe (PDF),
Rocketbook (RB), Mobipocket (PRC) & HTML

Edited by: *Brianna St. James*
Cover art by: *Syneca*

Warning:

The following material contains graphic sexual content meant for mature readers. *Chains of Love: Bound to Trust* has been rated *E-rotic* by a minimum of three independent reviewers.

Ellora's Cave Publishing offers three levels of Romantica™ reading entertainment: S (S-ensuous), E (E-rotic), and X (X-treme).

S-*ensuous* love scenes are explicit and leave nothing to the imagination.

E-*rotic* love scenes are explicit, leave nothing to the imagination, and are high in volume per the overall word count. In addition, some E-rated titles might contain fantasy material that some readers find objectionable, such as bondage, submission, same sex encounters, forced seductions, etc. E-rated titles are the most graphic titles we carry; it is common, for instance, for an author to use words such as "fucking", "cock", "pussy", etc., within their work of literature.

X-*treme* titles differ from E-rated titles only in plot premise and storyline execution. Unlike E-rated titles, stories designated with the letter X tend to contain controversial subject matter not for the faint of heart.

BOUND OF TRUST
CHAINS OF LOVE

Jaci Burton

Dedication

To JenK. Thanks for the great ideas, especially for the special 'plug'. I love your imagination.

To Puawai. Thank you for being so thoroughly vicious. You know why. I'm very grateful. ;)

To Joy, whose beautiful green eyes inspired the creation of Marina.

To Sire Don. I can't thank you enough for your insights and willingness to answer all my dumb questions. And a huge thank you for your beautiful designs.

To my wonderful editor, Briana St. James, who had a freaking brilliant series title idea. What would I do without you? ;)

And as always, to Charlie, for giving me all that I've ever asked for, and allowing me to give all that I am. You have my trust, and my love, for eternity.

Chapter One

Marina quickened her steps toward her superior's office, wondering why she'd been summoned. Laren had said it was important—a case that needed immediate assistance. Her heart sped up with excitement as it always did when she was assigned a new case. And she knew Laren was aware that she wanted more high-profile cases to work on.

Maybe today was the day.

She stepped into Laren's office and touched the pad to close the door. Her superior was on the private communicator, the combination ear and voice device giving her freedom to pace back and forth in the confined space. Always a bundle of nervous energy, Laren rarely stood still for long. She motioned for Marina to sit down, then quickly ended her call.

"Sorry. The tech group is coming in for system upgrades next week," Laren said, rolling her eyes. "As if I have time for shit like that."

Marina laughed at the incongruity of Laren's manner and appearance. Petite, with violet eyes and beautiful sable hair, Laren looked more like a young girl than a woman in her mid-thirties. Yet when she spoke, she commanded respect. Tops in this division, she knew galaxy law enforcement better than anyone Marina had ever met.

Laren was the best director she'd ever worked for. Tough, dedicated, and always fair. During her ten years with the Interplanetary Enforcement Unit, Marina had experienced her share of really bad superiors. The past two years with Laren at the helm had been nirvana. Not only was Laren a great boss, but they'd also become friends. Only a year apart in age, they quickly discovered they had much in common and socialized often.

There was always something to talk about. Mostly about being single women in a very tough field. And not wanting to get involved with men they worked with, which really limited their choices.

"So what's up?"

Laren sighed and sat at her desk, handing an electronic file to Marina. "You've been following the kidnappings, I assume."

Marina nodded and scanned the handheld device containing the case files. "Yeah. Been wanting to get in on this one for awhile now. Does this mean I'm assigned?"

Laren sat back in her chair and offered a half-smile, her violet eyes sparkling like amethysts. "Yes, if you're interested in the assignment. You may not want it."

There wasn't a job in the force too daunting for Marina. "Of course I want it. I've been itching to work this case. Tell me."

"One of our contacts in the Meloxian galaxy spied one of the missing girls on the planet Xarta. Since then, we've found out that two other missing Earth women have been seen on Xarta, which means at least three of them are on that planet. We think they've been taken there and sold as slaves to the Doms."

Marina arched a brow. Xarta was a known BDSM planet. She'd never visited there, since bondage and submission stuff wasn't her idea of fun sex. "I thought the planet bred submissive females. What do they need to go off-planet for?"

"The native females are submissive. And some women from other planets go to Xarta voluntarily to become submissives. But we've tracked the missing women, and we know of at least three who reside there now. Presumably against their will."

"So why can't we go get them and bring them back?"

"Our treaty with that galaxy forbids direct involvement unless we have probable cause. And we can't confirm that these women were kidnapped until we hear it directly from them. We'll have to get to them to find out."

"Is it possible they may have gone there willingly?"

Laren shrugged. "It's possible, but doubtful. The facts indicate kidnapping. They all disappeared around the same vicinity."

"Isn't that cause enough to go in there and talk to them?"

"Not according to the treaty. Their laws are quite different than ours and they're not too fond of Earth's interference anyway. They think we're bullies."

Marina snorted. "That's the pot calling the kettle black, isn't it? What do you want me to do?"

Laren leaned forward, clasping her hands together. "How do you feel about becoming a submissive?"

Marina's first thought was to laugh out loud, but she quickly realized Laren wasn't joking. "I don't really know how I feel about that. You know me, Laren. I'm the tough one, the one who eats men for breakfast—and I don't mean sexually, either."

She had a reputation as a ball-buster, a weapon-toting bitch who didn't take shit from anyone, especially the men she worked with. On the job they were professional, backing each other up. But Marina let them know she wasn't interested in getting involved personally. So most of them avoided her socially, which suited her just fine. She didn't need a man to make her complete, and obviously they were looking for the frilly feminine type anyway. Which sure as hell wasn't her.

At five-foot-nine, she was taller than average. Her body wasn't willowy and petite, either. She had big boobs, big hips and a big ass.

"You're the best investigator on the force, Marina. If anyone can do this job, you can."

"Tell me what you have in mind."

"I need you to put yourself in position to be kidnapped. We know the general vicinity where it occurs. It's within the party district in San Francisco. Three of the women were taken from the same club, two others from another club, and one from a BDSM club."

"So you want me to hang out at these places, hoping they'll take me?" Fat chance of that happening, considering she'd scanned the photos of the women who'd been taken. They were slender with perfect bodies. That simply wasn't her.

"Yes. I think if you act willing, they'll grab you in a heartbeat."

She snorted. "I'm hardly the type that a Dom will want."

Laren grinned. "Yes, you are. Or you will be. We have someone on the inside who will 'request' a female with your physical makeup."

"Inside?"

"Yeah. One of the interplanetary marshals is a native of Xarta. He'll be here today to go over the case with us. He's agreed to work undercover so that we can figure out who's taking the women on this end, and who's controlling it on the other end."

"You mean a Dom?"

"Yes. His name is Kaden, a native Dom from Xarta. But he doesn't live there any longer. He hasn't for years."

"Why not?"

Laren shrugged. "You'd have to ask him that question."

Marina shifted in the chair. She'd taken every assignment, no matter how dangerous or distasteful it was. She loved her job. But going undercover as a submissive? That meant giving a man control over her. Complete and utter control. For the first time, she wondered if she could handle a mission. "I'm not sure I can do this, Laren. I'm the last person in the world to be submissive to a man. I just don't fit the profile. I'm not meek; I don't bow or scrape to men. I see myself as an equal. I can't do this."

"Yes, you can."

"No way. They'd see right through me in a heartbeat."

"Remember, you wouldn't be a submissive when you got there. If you're kidnapped, you'd be fighting it. They'd expect you to fight it. You'd just have to learn how to be one."

"They'd never buy it."

"Of course they'd buy it. Both Kaden and I will help you acclimate yourself to the lifestyle. It's really not that difficult to study the behaviors of submissives. Plus, you wouldn't be a natural submissive. You'd be involuntarily brought there as a slave, so they wouldn't expect you to know how to act. The rest, Kaden can show you."

Marina shook her head, knowing that in this case, Laren was wrong. "I hate to disagree with my superior officer, Laren, but I'd never be able to pull it off."

Laren's lips curled into a teasing smile. "Marina, I'm a submissive."

Her mouth gaped open. "You?"

Laren nodded. "Yes. I've been a sub for quite some time."

"I never knew that. You don't seem the type."

"That's exactly the point. There is no such thing as 'type'. On Xarta, the women are expected to behave in a certain way, all the time. The submissive way. But here, it's different and always according to the agreement between an individual Dom and his or her sub.

"Being submissive is not always based on outward appearance or actions. And as you said, I don't 'look' like one. You and I are cut from the same cloth. Our parents were with the force. We grew up chewing nails instead of baby food. They made us tough, on the outside as well as the inside. But who you are in your job has no bearing on what you do in the bedroom."

Laren a submissive. She'd never have believed it. Where Marina was tough, Laren was tougher. Her exterior appearance belied her internal strength. "How can you be… I just don't get it." Marina smoothed back a wild curl that drooped over her eyes, completely shocked at this revelation.

"I love having control in my work and in my life. But sexually, I enjoy giving up that control to a man. Feeling his power, feeding his desires, is incredibly stimulating."

"Have you always been submissive?"

"Yes, but I didn't always know it. When I first became sexually active, I thought couples were equal in the bedroom. I demanded an equal partnership. Give and take, fifty-fifty. But I was never fulfilled. I always felt something was lacking in my sexual relationships. At first I thought I was choosing the wrong men. That is, until I met the right man—a Dom. Then I realized the problem all along had been with me, not the men. I wanted to be dominated, needed that special bond between me and a dominant male. Once I had that, there was no going back."

Marina had never been satisfied in the sex department, either. But her reasoning was because most men couldn't handle her. She had to give them instructions on what to do, how to do it. Otherwise she'd never have her needs met. She couldn't imagine giving herself up to a man's whims. Hell, she might as well give up sex then. "I'm glad you found what works for you. I hope it makes you happy."

"It did, for awhile anyway."

Marina studied Laren's faraway look and the sadness that darkened her eyes. "Something happened?"

Laren shook her head. "No big deal. I had a Dom who I thought I was in love with. But it didn't work out."

Marina guessed that it was more of a big deal than Laren let on, but she could tell Laren didn't want her to press for details. "I'm sorry."

Plastering on a smile that didn't quite match the dimness of her eyes, Laren said, "Thanks. Ancient history. Let's get back to the assignment. Do you think you can handle this?"

Could she? Could she act submissive, even undercover? Knowing it wasn't real would certainly help, but what did being a submissive entail? Would her normally dominant nature prevent her from doing her job?

Then again, it burned her ass that women were being taken against their will, especially to become slaves to some man's ideal of the perfect woman. Bastards. "I'm not sure if I'm cut out to be a submissive, but I guess if someone can train me then I'm game for this."

"Oh, I'll be able to train you. You don't need to worry."

She quickly stood and turned toward the distinctly male voice behind her.

Tall. *Really* tall. Six-foot-four at least. Just the kind of height she liked on a man. His body was her ideal, too. Broad shouldered, long legs, eyes the color of aged whiskey. Hair that was a little darker at the roots and golden blond the rest of the way, like someone who spent a lot of time at the beach. The kind of man a woman would look twice at when he walked by. Hell, more than twice. He was beautiful.

"Hello, Kaden, thanks for coming so quickly." Laren inclined her head toward Marina. "Kaden, this is Marina, the investigator I told you about."

He nodded, his sharp gaze assessing her from head to toe. She heated under his penetrating stare.

Marina was dumbfounded by her body's instant reaction to this man. She felt hot, sweaty and aroused. He looked human, at least the parts of him she could see. And he sure as hell didn't look like a marshal, dressed in tight black pants that hugged his muscular thighs and a plain T-shirt that showed off an impressively broad chest. She fixed her gaze on his face so her eyes wouldn't wander over parts of him that made her wonder if *all* of him was human.

"Kaden," she said, nodding back at him.

"You're beautiful," he said, his voice a seductive caress.

Shock and warmth spread through her at his deep voice. It carried an underlying sensuality that caused a chemical reaction inside her. Fighting the languorous effects of his presence, she asked, "Is that part of your standard line?"

He frowned. "Standard line?"

"Yeah. Tell a woman she's beautiful and she'll do whatever you want?"

He grinned. "No. That's not how it works." He looked over to Laren. "She has much to learn, doesn't she?"

"Yes," Laren replied. "But she'll learn quickly."

"Does she realize what this role will encompass?"

Nothing like being talked about as if she wasn't even there. "I'm right here, you know. You can address me directly."

Kaden glanced over at her with narrowed eyes. "If I meant to address you, I would have. Right now I'm talking to Laren."

When he turned away as if she'd been nothing more than a momentary distraction, steam boiled up within her. She wanted nothing more at that moment than to kick him between his oh-so-muscular legs and find out if his equipment was located in the same place as human men. Arrogant bastard!

"This training will not be easy. I'll need someone who's willing to accept my commands."

Over her dead body. "Now wait a minute. I didn't agree that you were in charge of this mission. Actually, I'm the one who should be—"

"This will never work," Kaden interrupted, continuing to address Laren as if Marina wasn't even present. "She's unwilling to accept training, let alone dominance."

Refusing to be dismissed, Marina said, "Look, Xartanian, I never once said that I was going to be either trained or dominated by you. In fact, I haven't agreed to do this mission. At least not yet. Although you're making it sound so incredibly appealing." If she wasn't an adult she'd have followed up her statement by sticking her tongue out at him.

"She has a smart mouth. There would be many punishments. I don't think she can handle it."

The words had been meant for her superior, but he finally looked over at Marina as he said them. His eyes darkened like a storm, pupils dilating. Punishments, at least to him, meant something sexual, and something clearly exciting to him.

But not to her, no matter how her body throbbed. Hell, she even felt this weird electrical jolt traveling from him to her, though they were more than three feet apart. What exactly did he mean by punishments? And why was her body suddenly firing on all cylinders, feeling charged and raring to go? Dammit!

Think about work, don't think about sex. Don't mentally undress him, Marina. He's trouble with a capital "T" and you know it. You know his type. You hate arrogant, smug men like him. Focus, focus, focus.

Laren looked at her. "You have to make the choice. Perhaps it would be helpful if you spent some time with Kaden this evening. A submissive on Xarta has very few rights other than to serve and please her Dom. Someone of your nature may not be able to handle it. And your performance as a submissive *must* be believable for this to work. The Doms on Xarta will see through you in a minute if it looks like you're acting the part instead of living it. You have to make it seem as if you fight it in the beginning, and then come around to the submissive way of life after a period of training."

Fighting it would be no problem at all. But the rest of it? This was all too much to decipher in one short conversation. First she had to fight, then she had to submit? Hell, how would she know what to do when?

She'd wanted this assignment for over a year. It was high-profile and could boost her career. She'd been a senior investigator for three years now, and was up for a promotion soon. Solving these interplanetary kidnappings could be the key to her success.

So she'd have to fake being a submissive for a period of time. So what? She could handle any assignment. She hadn't been taught to be tough so that the first time a difficult assignment came up she'd back off. No way.

"I'll do it. Don't worry about me. I can handle it."

"There will be sex. Actual sex, not simulated," Kaden said. "And the aforementioned punishments." His direct gaze challenged her.

She fought back the urge to say "hell no!", knowing that whatever it took to get the job done, she'd do. Instead, she shrugged as if it didn't matter. "Sex is no big deal. Whatever it takes to solve the disappearances of these women, I'm up for it."

"Are you sure, Marina?" Laren asked. "You can't change your mind once this starts. Once you're taken to Xarta we can't easily get you out of there. Kaden won't even be able to get you out without compromising himself in the process."

More determined than ever to show both Laren and Kaden that she could handle her job, she nodded. "I'm in. When do we get started?"

"Soon," Kaden answered. "But first you need to be briefed about what's going to happen. I want you to meet me for dinner tonight at my hotel."

"Why not here and now?"

"Because I'm starting your training this evening, and believe me, you don't want to do that in front of your peers."

What the hell did that mean? She looked to Laren, who smiled enigmatically and said, "It's now or never, Marina. If you accept, you'll take your orders from Kaden from here on out. I need to know if you can handle it because if not I have to find someone else fast."

Why did she hesitate? She'd never waffled over an assignment before, no matter how personal her involvement would be. So why now? Lifting her chin, she glared at Kaden and said, "I said I'm in. Where and when?"

"The Ilumia Hotel on Mission Street. Eight o'clock in the lobby."

She nodded and started to leave the office.

"And wear a dress," he added.

She halted and turned. "I don't think so."

"Wear a dress," he said again, his voice calm and even.

"I said no."

"One more time, Marina. Wear a dress."

His tone changed, adding an edge, a warning that indicated he wasn't happy. Good. Pissing him off on a regular basis might be the most enjoyable aspect of this assignment. "Why?"

"Because your training starts tonight and you need to start following my orders. So far it's not looking good."

Sonofabitch! Had he just set her up? She looked to Laren, who wore a very worried expression on her face. Her superior officer had never once doubted her abilities to complete an assignment. "Fine," she said, gritting her teeth as she choked the words out. "Eight o'clock."

"In a dress."

Dickhead. "Yes, dammit. In a dress."

Before she could utter the invectives she wanted to fling at the arrogant alien, she left Laren's office, deciding to call it a day and work off her irritation in the exercise room at home. By the time eight o'clock came around, she might have her temper under control.

Then again, she might not. They weren't in Xarta so she didn't have to turn into a pussycat just yet. She might just have to show Kaden what kind of partner he'd be dealing with on this assignment.

Oh hell. First she had to stop at the store and buy a fucking dress.

* * * * *

"She's quite something, isn't she?" Kaden said, sliding into the chair that Marina vacated. He still felt her presence, smelled her unique female scent as if she'd actually touched him.

Which she hadn't. He'd remedy that soon enough.

Laren smirked. "Yes, she is. You held back admirably. What do you think?"

"I think she'll be difficult." And his body was more than up to the challenge, as it had been the moment she'd turned around and he'd gotten his first look at her.

Dark, smoldering sexuality simmered within Marina. Her eyes, emerald windows as glittery as the green seas of Xarta, were the most prominent feature on her face. Her skin was a soft, buttery caramel that he itched to touch and taste. And that hair of hers—wild, wavy, with a sensuality all its own. She tried to tame it by winding it into a knot at the back of her head. Oh no, that wouldn't do at all. She would wear her hair down, curling along her shoulders and over her breasts, available for him to tangle his fingers within or wrap around his fist and tug while he fucked her.

His cock drew hard and tight against his pants, the first time he'd felt instantaneous sexual stirrings for a woman in far too long.

"She'll do her job, Kaden. And she'll do it well."

But would she learn to do him as well? He'd read the challenge that simmered in her magical green eyes, making them glitter like hard emeralds. But something else showed on her face, something she didn't even know she possessed.

A desire to be dominated. He knew it. Felt it, deep within. She might think she was the dominant one, but he'd soon show her she had no control at all.

Not where it counted. And she'd *want* him to take over. "Will she be receptive?" he asked Laren, knowing his old friend would know whether Marina could handle the lifestyle.

"Honestly? I have no idea. She'll do her job and she'll act accordingly, of course. But as far as whether she'll truly accept you as her Dom, I don't know, Kaden. I wish I did, but I can't give you one hundred percent certainty."

"I know you can't. It's good enough that you've recommended her, Laren. I'm sure she'll be fine, especially after my training."

Laren laughed. "I can only imagine. If only I could be a fly on the wall and watch the way you two interact. I'd pay big money to see that event."

After he left Laren's office, he went back to his hotel, tossed his things on the spacious bed and climbed into the water-based shower device. At least they still used water here instead of the antibacterial cleansing rituals some of the other planets had.

As he showered he thought of Marina. Laren couldn't guarantee that Marina would be cooperative. He didn't need Laren's guarantee anyway. Just being near Marina allowed him to connect with her on a psychic level. While he couldn't read her mind, he could pick up on her emotions. She showed much more through her expressive eyes than she knew, and what he'd read led him to believe she wasn't as repulsed at the thought of submission as she wanted him to believe.

Then again, theirs wouldn't be a usual Dom/sub relationship either. She wasn't going into this wanting to become a submissive. If all went as planned, she'd be kidnapped, prepared and put on the auction block. She'd be an unwilling slave, something he found distasteful, yet seemed to be a lifestyle his planet embraced now. It wasn't enough that the born and bred Xartanian women were more than eager to submit to their Dom. No, the controllers of the planet also had to indulge those who wanted the unwilling women.

Ten years ago, he'd refused to play the part of slave owner of an unwilling female. Yet he'd also grown bored with the Xartanian-born women who offered him no challenge. He was fucked either choice he made, and not in a satisfying way.

What the hell did he want? A willing or unwilling woman? That question he'd spent the better part of ten years trying to answer.

But he already knew. He wanted a woman who was his equal outside of the bedroom, his slave within. The type of woman he would never meet among the native females of Xarta. The kind of woman he craved went against his own biological makeup. He was supposed to want a willing sub, not one who would challenge him in all areas except sexually.

And that type of woman wasn't easy to find. Laren was one, in fact had fallen in love with one of his friends. A friend who had walked away from Laren as if she meant nothing to him. Kaden knew the real reasons, but he wouldn't interfere. It wasn't his place to get in the middle of a Dom and his sub. He felt Laren's sorrow though, and wished he could comfort her.

His thoughts strayed to Marina and what kind of submissive she could be. She was certainly a dominant female, at least in her work. But what would she be like sexually? Did she want to dominate her men in the bedroom, too?

Instinct told him no. Then again, he could be completely wrong about her. Either way, he'd have her on his terms, whether she liked it or not.

What did it matter anyway? He'd play his part, and she'd play hers. Only it would be a game, a charade where neither of them was seriously intending to further their relationship.

When they uncovered those responsible for the kidnappings and their mission was over, Marina would come back to Earth and resume her life, and he'd go back to patrolling the galaxies.

Pity.

Then again, she would be his to train for as long as the mission lasted. And as long as it lasted, he'd enjoy every moment of her submission.

Chapter Two

A dress. Stupid fucking dress. Marina hated wearing them, preferring the comfort of her uniform pants and jacket with a light shirt underneath. Which is why she had to go shopping after she left work. She didn't even own a dress. She wore pants. All the time. She could move, kick, be mobile in pants. In this getup she was lucky to be able to walk. High heels should be a Dom's torture device. Insanity must have taken hold of her today when she'd let the sales woman con her into these ridiculous shoes.

She slipped out of the transport vehicle and gave the driver her card to charge the required credits for the trip. Sucking in a breath of courage, she strolled to the front door, watching her reflection in the glass as she approached. The black dress fit snug, showing off her curves. A little tight in the bust, her cleavage swelled over the bodice more than she preferred. What did she know about buying dresses, anyway? She'd been desperate to get out of the store, and the saleswoman had been *very* persuasive. Marina had finally given up and let the expert choose for her.

The heels, vicious devices of pain that they were, made her legs look long and slender. She'd pulled her hair into a clip, but the stiff breeze whipped curling tendrils free, the unruly strands tickling her face.

Ah well. It would just have to do. She still wondered why she'd worn this getup. Just because Kaden asked her to? She was really going to hate this assignment.

Kaden was waiting for her in the middle of the lobby, hands clasped behind his back and wearing a no-nonsense, straight face. He didn't crack a smile as she approached.

In fact, he didn't speak at all when she stopped in front of him, just continued to stare at her, tilting his head to the side as he looked the length of her. Finally, he said, "Nice dress. Thank you for wearing it."

Shock caused her momentary speechlessness. He thanked her? "You're welcome."

He turned and walked away. Obviously she was supposed to follow him like some obedient servant. If this was the way he treated his first dates, she'd bet he didn't get many second ones. Not that they were dating. Oh hell, she didn't know where her mind was.

They were escorted to a semi-circular booth in a corner of the restaurant, lit only by candles. When Marina slid into the booth along the corner wall, Kaden slipped in next to her. The more she scooted over, the more he followed. Short of falling on her ass onto the floor, she had to make do with the fact he was going to sit right next to her.

The waiter approached and waited for their order. Kaden took a brief look at the menu on the monitor behind them, then ordered wine and both their dinners. The waiter smiled and hurried off before Marina could get a chance to object.

"I'm perfectly capable of ordering my own drink and food."

"You might as well get over that. From now on, I'll be telling you what to eat and drink, among other things."

Irritation swept through her. So this was how it was going to be, with him controlling her every move and making all the decisions for her. And Laren enjoyed this shit?

"Look, Kaden. Let's get one thing clear right now. I'm doing this because it's my job. Not because I want to be dominated or am in any way interested in this lifestyle. Got it?"

He didn't respond, just grinned at her.

Prick. She hoped this would be a very short assignment.

Their wine arrived and Kaden poured a glass for her. She had half a mind to ignore it, but what the hell. After taking a sip, she had to admit it was fantastic. Smooth, mellow, not too sweet or bitter. Just the way she liked it. "This is good."

"Yes, I knew you'd like it."

She rolled her eyes, hoping he wouldn't notice. What, was he psychic, too?

"Let's talk about what's going to happen," he said.

At least one of them could concentrate. "Okay."

"Once you're taken, you will be brought into a preparation room. There, you'll be stripped, bathed, and readied for auction."

"How appealing. I can't wait."

Ignoring her sarcasm, he continued. "At auction, you will be showcased for potential buyers. I'll be one of them, and I'll be purchasing you."

She refused to think that he might be the only one bidding on her. "Fine."

"Once I purchase you, this game begins. There are some things you won't find pleasant, considering your nature."

She looked at him. "Such as?"

He reached for a curl of her hair and wound it around his fingers. When she started to jerk away, he held her firm.

"Such as this. I'll be touching you. Anyway I want to, anywhere I want to. You can fight, of course, but I'll make you obey."

"You can bet your ass I'll fight you." No one told her what to do. Ever.

"That's good. They'll expect that. But don't fight too hard or for too long or they'll dispose of you. A little bit of a wildcat is a good thing, especially during the auction because that brings about high bids. Too much fight and they'll think you untrainable."

He was making this sound more and more alluring by the second. "I'll try to keep that in mind. What happens after that?"

"As your Dom, I'll be chaining you to me and leading you to the privacy chamber where we'll get…acquainted."

She watched his expression, but he revealed nothing of what he was thinking or feeling. "You mean we'll fuck."

His light chuckle was unnerving. "There's a lot more to it than just fucking. Remember, as my submissive, your primary reason for existence is to please me. And you *will* please me."

Was that a threat or confidence? Emotions warred within her. She wanted to be pissed off at his arrogant attitude, and yet the way he spoke with such assurance that she would "please him" gave her a thrill she hadn't expected to feel. "Exactly what kind of 'pleasing' will I do?"

He picked up his wine glass and swirled the liquid around the glass. She studied his long fingers, imagining what they'd feel like against her skin and inside her. Before her imagination went too far, she blinked to shake off the erotic thoughts.

"The kind of pleasing I'm in the mood for at the moment."

"Such as?"

He tilted his head. "You seem fascinated by what I'm going to do to you, Marina. Are you anxious to begin your training?"

"No!" She realized as soon as she shouted the word that she was protesting more than she should. "I mean, I'd just like to be forewarned about what could happen. If I'm going to be flogged, I'd like to mentally prepare myself."

Tucking the errant curl behind her ear, he traced her earlobe with his finger. She shivered at the warmth of his touch. "I don't want you to know ahead of time what I'm going to do. It will be more pleasurable for me if you don't know."

She snorted. "Pleasurable for you is the key, isn't it?"

"What pleases me, Marina, will also please you."

She looked away and stared into her wine. "I doubt that."

He reached for her chin and turned her head to face him. "You doubt that I can pleasure you?"

She smirked. "Many have tried. Few have succeeded."

"Then you've been with the wrong men."

Tell her something she didn't know. As far as she was concerned, there was no *right* man. Either that or she was just impossible to please.

Determined to get off the subject of sex and pleasure, she said, "So tell me about yourself, Kaden."

"I'd rather talk about you." He shifted closer and rested his arm over the back of the booth. The hairs of his forearm tickled the back of her neck and she leaned forward to avoid his touch.

Damn, he smelled good too. Some kind of musk, but it wasn't cologne. Whatever his scent was, it was unique to him and filled her mind with thoughts of passion. There was something elementally arousing about a man who smelled good. Yet with Kaden, his scent wasn't manufactured cologne. It seemed to emanate from his body as if it were natural. Pheromones, maybe? Trying to be subtle about it, she inhaled deeply and closed her eyes. When she opened them, he was staring at her.

A woman could get lost in eyes like his. She quickly looked away.

"I asked you to tell me about yourself," he said again, his voice low, almost near a whisper.

"Not much to tell. I've been an investigator with the enforcement unit for ten years."

"How old are you?"

"Thirty-four." She looked to him. "You?"

His smile made her heart slam against her chest. "We don't age the same as you. But if you had to calculate it by your Earth years, I'm in my early forties."

He had a dimple on one side of his mouth, right where his lips curved upward into that devastating smile. His scent kept drawing her, making her want to lean against him and run her tongue along his skin to find out if he tasted as good as he smelled. She blinked and sat back, taking a long swallow of wine. Kaden refilled her glass.

"Lift your dress to your thighs," he said.

Her eyes widened. Surely she hadn't heard him right. "Excuse me?"

"Lift your dress. I want to see your legs."

"Are you insane? I'm not doing that here. We're in public!" Even if her body woke with a vengeance at his suggestion. She wished now that she'd had sex recently. It was just being close to a man again after so long that made her nerve endings vibrate.

He moved his hand to her shoulder, lazily playing with the silk sleeve. "When I tell you to do something, Marina, I will expect you to obey without question. Any time you question me or refuse to do what I ask, you will be punished."

"Why?"

"Because it's what I want. As my slave, you will be obligated to do anything I ask of you."

"So you can humiliate me? Do you get off on that?"

He frowned and shook his head. "Of course not. I would never do anything to cause you to suffer humiliation. You don't understand the concept of dominants and submissives. You need to understand one thing—whatever I do to you is for my pleasure, but also for yours."

"So you said. You really think I'll enjoy all this?"

"Why don't you let me demonstrate? Cooperate completely with me through dinner tonight, and then you decide whether you derive any pleasure from it."

This would be her chance to prove him wrong. "You're on."

"You must promise to do whatever I ask, no matter what it is."

"Now wait a minute—"

He held up his hand to silence her. "Remember that I will never do anything to humiliate you. On that you have my word."

What did she have to lose? Let the high and mighty master prove himself. "Okay, let's play."

One corner of his mouth curved upward, revealing that dimple. His eyes darkened and he said, "Lift your dress to your thighs."

Marina looked around the restaurant. No one was sitting in the nearby booths. In fact, not a single person was paying any attention to them. Besides, the tablecloth draped to the floor, hiding her legs. The only one seeing them would be Kaden. Feeling more nervous than she should, she reached down and laid her hands in her lap, then slowly drew the silk dress above her knees, stopping short of revealing her thighs completely.

"I said to your thighs."

She looked at him, and his dark eyes mesmerized her. There was something so hot about the way they seemed to change color from the brightest summer sky to the darkest stormy cloud. But still, the way he commanded her was annoying as hell.

"This is high enough."

"Lift it all the way to the tops of your thighs. Don't argue with me."

She was about to do just that when she realized that Kaden held the key to this assignment. If she failed in this little task, her could easily go back to Laren and claim that Marina wasn't going to work out.

So big deal. Do it. It doesn't matter, anyway. The important thing is the assignment. Think promotion, and don't think about anything else.

With a resigned sigh, she lifted the dress higher, revealing her thighs.

"You have beautiful legs."

No, she didn't. Her thighs were large. Firm from all the exercise she did, but not pencil thin like a lot of other women. She didn't possess the body type attractive to most men. Why did that matter, anyway? What did she care what Kaden thought of her thighs? This was a job, and nothing more.

"Are you wearing panties, Marina?"

"Yes."

"Slide them off."

"What?" Surely he wasn't suggesting she give him a little striptease in the corner of the restaurant.

"Take them off. And don't make me repeat myself again, or you'll be punished."

"Yeah, right. What could you possibly do to me here to punish me?"

"Obey me, or I'll turn you over my knee and give the restaurant patrons a little glimpse of your naked ass while I spank you."

"You wouldn't."

He arched a brow. "Try me."

Would he really do that? Surely not. Then again, aliens very often had different views of what constituted an embarrassing situation. He probably would have no qualms about baring her ass and spanking her in the middle of the room.

Her cunt quivered at the mental image.

The look in his eyes indicated he was dead serious. Ignoring the tingling between her legs, she lifted her dress. Heat spread over her face at being put into this position, and she mentally damned Kaden for forcing her into this. She had half a mind to stand up and walk out of the restaurant, mission be damned. Instead, she reached for her panties, pulled them over her knees and down her legs. When they were off, she wadded them in her fist.

"Give them to me."

She hesitated at first, but he continued to glare at her, so she handed them over. He slipped them into his pocket and took a sip of his wine.

A simple act, and yet showing his possession of her. He had her panties, which she supposed was a form of Dom control over his sub. She hadn't done as much research as she would have liked to, but she had spent a little time going over the dominant and submissive relationship on her computer at home.

Marina had to admit that sitting there with no panties on and her dress pulled up almost to her crotch was amazingly stimulating. The cool air caressed her slit and her pussy quivered with excitement. Creamy arousal pooled between her legs, the decadent feeling of doing something she shouldn't be doing making her cunt spasm with anticipation.

She'd never had a man play intimate games with her before. Sex had been reserved for the bedroom and had been more perfunctory than arousing. This was…different, and not in a bad way. Her body had awakened to new sensations, her mind following suit and thinking very naughty thoughts.

Her vibrator was going to be in for a treat tonight.

"Let me see your pussy," he said, turning sideways in the booth so that he faced her.

Marina sucked in a breath, trying not to show how his words affected her. "I don't think so."

He sighed. "Are we going to do this all night? I give the command and you argue? It can't work this way on Xarta. You're either in this assignment or you're out. I can easily contact Laren and get someone else—"

"Fine," she hissed, angry as hell that he played that trump card. "I'll do it." She looked around the restaurant to be sure no one was watching, then subtly pulled the dress higher, revealing her pussy. Her nipples beaded and pressed against her silk bra, the contact of skin to satin like a soft caress.

Kaden looked down. His chest rose with his intake of breath, his eyelids half closing as he inhaled. "I can smell you. Sweet, like vanilla. Musky, like a woman in the depths of heavy arousal." He opened his eyes and met her gaze.

Marina swallowed and tried to think clearly. Clarity was damned difficult with the way Kaden was looking at her. He smiled and she wanted to dissolve, liquefy and slide under the table into a puddle. The air in the restaurant had suddenly become stifling hot and she found it hard to breathe. Her pussy went into pulsing spasms of uncontrollable desire, her juices seeping along her inner thigh.

This wasn't supposed to be turning her on!

"I'm going to touch you," he said, and her eyes widened, but this time she didn't respond.

What could she say? There was no point in denying she was more aroused than she'd ever been before. He laid his hand on her thigh, sliding it toward her aching slit. She sucked her bottom lip between her teeth and fought the urge to beg him to hurry.

His hand was hot against her skin, his palm rough as he moved along her inner thigh as if he had all the time in the world to explore her. Marina glanced up to see the waiter approaching them with a tray in hand. She quickly pulled her dress down and made to move away.

"Don't move," Kaden said.

"The waiter's coming!" she whispered back, clenching her legs together so he'd get the hint and remove his hand.

"The waiter can't see what I'm doing. Now relax and smile at him."

Her thighs trembled as the waiter approached. Kaden continued to tease her inner thigh, drawing ever closer to her aroused flesh. Despite the fear of discovery, the fact he continued to touch her was like a jolt of wicked lightening, so exciting she was afraid she'd come before he ever reached her pot of gold.

Apparently oblivious to what was happening under her dress, the waiter deposited their food on the table and asked if there'd be anything else. Her mind whispered, *yes, an orgasm would be nice*, but she quickly shook her head and stifled a gasp as Kaden's fingers brushed her mound.

After the waiter left, Marina squeezed her legs together, trapping Kaden's hand between her thighs. "Kaden, dinner's here."

"Then eat," he replied, his fingers traveling higher.

How was she supposed to eat when he was doing such delicious things to her body? Her appetite had shifted from hunger for food to starvation for what his fingers could do to her.

"I said eat." He picked up his fork with his right hand, still exploring her slit with his free hand, dipping his fingers into the nectar spilling from her cunt.

She picked up her fork and put a few bites into her mouth, but she couldn't concentrate on eating. Hell, she didn't even know *what* she was eating! How could she focus on anything but the way Kaden touched her sex? She let out a gasp when he circled her clit, drawing her juices over the distended nub and slowly caressing her. She forced the fork back in her mouth, then moaned when he slid one finger inside her.

He continued to swirl his fingers over her sex, occasionally dipping one finger inside her. All the while, he continued to eat as if he wasn't paying the slightest attention to the turmoil he was causing between her legs. Marina couldn't eat a bite of food. Her appetite had definitely trained itself in a different direction.

"You're hot," he said, laying his fork down on his empty plate. "And very wet."

She was also extremely close to coming, and if he kept fucking her with his finger she'd have an orgasm in less than a minute.

But he withdrew, and slid his finger between his lips, drawing her nectar into his mouth. "You taste like hot sex.

I'd love to crawl between your legs and lick you until you poured more of that sweet juice into my mouth, Marina. Tell me, would you like that?"

Despite the fact they were in a public place, she wanted nothing more than to feel his hot mouth on her aching sex, lapping up her cream until she screamed so loud the kitchen help would hear her. Of course he wouldn't do that, so there was no harm in telling him how much she really wanted that to happen. "Yes."

He dabbed his mouth with the napkin and pushed the table away from the booth a few inches. Her jaw dropped when he slipped down under the table and pulled her knees apart.

Oh my God! "Kaden, get up! What are you doing?" she said, hoping she was whispering as opposed to the shrieking, shocked voice she heard in her own head.

"I'm giving you what you want. Remember this when I ask you to do something for me."

"Get out of there! You can't..."

Her words were lost as he pulled her ass forward, aligning her aching cunt with the edge of the cushioned booth. He leaned between her thighs and took a long, slow lick along her slit.

She tensed and tried to scoot away, but he held tight to her thighs. She had a choice now. Force the issue and scream if she had to, thereby causing no end to the embarrassment she'd suffer, or let him do whatever he wanted.

Dammit, neither of those were good choices.

"Kaden, don't. Please get out of there."

He looked up at her, his fingers caressing the skin of her thighs. "You will quickly learn that you have no say so in what I do. I do what I please, when I please. Just relax and enjoy it, Marina."

Sit back and enjoy it? She'd never be able to do that. She'd have to keep an eye on everyone around her while trying to hold in the moans that he was already causing. There was no way she was going to enjoy—

Oh, dear God in heaven!

Marina could only shudder and fight back the moans that threatened to escape her lips. Kaden's tongue was magical, his mouth heaven on earth as he sucked her clit, gently tugging the nub until all she could see were the sparks of pleasure.

She peeked down and watched him stroke and lick her, sliding his tongue inside her throbbing cunt to lap up the juices she couldn't seem to control. He lifted his eyes and met her gaze, holding her as if he commanded that she watch. He shifted, raised his hand alongside his mouth and plunged two fingers inside her pussy. She whimpered, then coughed to hide the sound.

Somewhere in the recesses of her mind she wondered if anyone was watching, then finally decided she didn't care. Let them watch. She was seconds from coming, lifting her hips now to drive her sex against Kaden's mouth. Pressure built within her at his relentless strokes, his tongue and mouth creating a vortex of sensations she could no longer manage.

Kaden had the control—all of it. She could do nothing but sit there and give herself to him, acquiescing to his unspoken demands. With every swipe of his tongue, every thrust of his fingers, he controlled her. His mastery of her body was shocking. No man could ever get her off without explicit instructions, yet he played her as if he knew every intimate part of her body.

She couldn't take it anymore. Holding her fist against her mouth, she bit down to quiet the screams that bubbled in the back of her throat as her climax hit her hard and furious. Her legs shook, her ass pumped up and down in time to the rhythmic strokes of Kaden's tongue. He drank up all the juices she spilled until she had nothing left to give him. Spent, she remained in the same wanton position he'd put her in as he eased back up and took his place next to her. In fact, he was the one who smoothed her skirt down over her legs and gently pulled her upright. She couldn't have done it. Whether from shock or utter satisfaction, she felt like a bowl of gelatin.

She'd never given herself like that to a man before. Never. She'd always called the shots. Told them where to touch her, how to fuck her. And even then, she hadn't come.

Her first experience with Kaden, in a restaurant no less, and she'd had the best orgasm she could remember having. And she'd had very little say so in how that orgasm had come about. The realization left her more than a little uncomfortable.

Kaden took a long drink of his wine, then turned to her. "Now you understand, at least the beginning. You were very good to do as I said. Get used to it."

She looked down and saw his raging erection pressed firmly against his pants. It was long and thick and made her mouth crave a taste of him.

His gaze followed hers and when she looked up at him, he smiled. "You'll have plenty of chances to pleasure me. In fact, very soon that's all you'll be doing. Everything you do on Xarta will be for my pleasure and my pleasure alone."

She should tell him she'd do nothing at all for his pleasure, but right now he was right—she'd do pretty much anything he asked of her. That mind-blowing orgasm he'd given her was like nothing she'd ever experienced.

As if he'd been paid to stay away, their waiter suddenly reappeared and asked if they wanted dessert. Marina smiled and shook her head, thinking she'd already had the best post-dinner delight of her life.

"Tomorrow night we'll set you up to begin haunting the locations of the kidnappings. If all goes well, it won't be long until you're taken. I'll be heading to Xarta tonight to reestablish myself in my home city. Once there I'll contact the auctioneers and let them know I'm seeking out a new submissive. I'll specifically ask for someone with your beauty and exotic looks."

Beauty? Exotic looks? Her? She refused to be complimented by his description of her. In fact, she refused to be moved at all by the blond-haired alien who oozed sex from his pores. She was tough. She could take this, and she absolutely, positively would never submit to him in her reality. The minimum required—that's all he'd get from her.

And if she received a few more earth-shattering orgasms like the one he just gave her, she'd consider that a perk of the job.

Chapter Three

For two nights Marina had set herself up as a kidnap wannabe, only to discover no one wanted to kidnap her. How embarrassing.

She'd spent the first night strolling around two of the suspected clubs. Oh sure, she'd been offered drinks and danced with a few of the guys, but nothing else happened. No one had asked her out. Not that she'd have said yes, but it would have been nice to have been asked, dammit.

One more night of hitting the clubs in this stupid outfit and she'd scream. High heels—again—along with a skirt that was too tight and too short. The skin-tight top accentuated her large breasts. Laren should be shot for forcing her into this getup. She was uncomfortable and out of her element. In fact, she looked like a woman desperate to find a man. The whole scenario was revolting.

She surveyed the BDSM club she'd ventured into for tonight's wasted effort, convinced that no one was going to kidnap her no matter what type of woman Kaden asked for. The club was a single room packed with people dressed in all manners of bondage gear, from tight leather to cuffs, bars, masks and chains. Then there were those dressed normally, and of course the ones who were stark naked except for the collar and leash binding them to their masters. Interestingly, there were both male and female submissives. With a snort, she wondered if any of the male submissives were men she'd slept with, because the guys in her past certainly had no idea how to take the initiative.

Too bad she didn't have more time to ask each person what the hell they were wearing and why. She'd wager she'd get quite an education in a place like this. Then again, if all went as planned and she ended up a slave on Xarta, she'd probably get much more enlightened than she wanted to.

The other night in the restaurant with Kaden already seemed like a distant dream, something that happened only in her imagination. She wasn't that kind of girl, silly as that sounded. Normally she'd never allow a man to dominate her so completely, do things to her that she'd never dream of doing in public. And yet she'd been completely pliable in Kaden's hands. Her body thrummed with awakening desire at the remembered feel of his soft tongue against her clit. She'd about fallen out of the booth at the first touch of his wet mouth against her aching slit. But the most amazing thing about that night was that she had come. For years she'd tried to show men the roadmap to pleasing her, with no success.

Until Kaden. He'd rocketed her into an orgasm so easily, when no man had ever been able to do that before. Her thoughts lingered on what it would be like to fuck him, to wrap her legs tight around him and pull his cock deep into her throbbing pussy.

Kaden was a dangerous man. A dangerous man who had influenced her when she was in a weakened condition. She frowned as she remembered that condition—her skirt hiked up to her hips and his face buried between her legs. Yes, she'd have to watch herself around him.

That is, if she ever saw him again. At the rate she was going, she'd be pulled off this case within the next twenty-four hours and replaced with a younger, thinner, more attractive investigator.

And wouldn't that just look great on her work record? Fat, unattractive unit officer pulled off case for utter failure to be enticing.

Ugh.

"Thirsty?"

She turned at the sound of a distinctly female voice. A young woman stood in front of her. Couldn't be more than mid-twenties. Blonde, blue-eyed perfect specimen of woman. Big breasts, small waist and long legs. The last person Marina should be standing next to. She looked like a bronze hippo next to this creature.

"Hi. My name is Marina."

"I'm Rora," the blonde said, dropping her eyes as she spoke.

A submissive movement, no doubt. Lord this woman was gorgeous. "Nice to meet you, Rora."

"Thank you," she said with a smile, peeking through her lashes at Marina. "I saw you standing here alone and thought you might like a drink."

Hard to believe that a woman like this would be wanting to hang out with Marina, considering the amount of men currently salivating in their direction. "Sure, I'd love one."

Rora handed her a glass filled with a red mixture. "Try this. It's a combination I put together myself and tastes very good."

Marina accepted the glass and asked, "Do you work here?"

"Off and on. Tonight I'm off but wanted to stop in and see what was happening. It's very busy."

She followed Rora's gaze to the people jammed together. "Yes, it is."

Marina took a sip of the dark liquid, pleasantly surprised by its tangy flavor. "This is good!"

Rora grinned. "One of my favorites. I'm glad you like it."

Studying the beauty standing next to her, Marina couldn't fathom why she'd be without a man, especially since her stance and facial expressions led her to believe that Rora was a submissive. "Do you have a sire?"

"Oh yes."

Knowing that submissives were not often allowed anywhere without their Doms keeping close watch over them, she asked, "And you're here unescorted?"

A slight blush tinged her pale cheeks. "He's here. He asked me to come over and talk to you."

Marina arched a brow. "Really? Why?"

"He finds you very attractive and wants to meet you."

Rora's Dom had to be blind. Why would he want Marina when the perfect woman already belonged to him? But since she was supposed to mingle, she figured this was a start, especially if Rora and her Dom were regulars. "Really?"

"Yes. You are such a contrast to me. He wondered if you would agree to dance with me. It would please him to see us together."

Ah. Rora's Dom wanted to fix Marina up with Rora. Not really her type, even if she was an incredibly beautiful woman. Marina's sexual desires had never leaned toward other women, even though she'd fantasized about same-sex encounters now and then while masturbating.

Oh, what the hell. Maybe if the slavers were somewhere in attendance, she could make herself more visible this way. "Sure. I'd love to."

Marina finished her drink and sat it on the bar counter, then followed Rora to the crowded dance floor. The song playing had a fast, driving beat and Rora began to gyrate to the enticing music. Admittedly, the song was one of Marina's favorites. She turned it on in her apartment all the time and danced around while doing her cleaning and laundry. She soon found herself swept into the rhythm, picking up the way Rora moved and dancing in time to the woman's actions. Rora's breasts swelled tight against her flimsy silk top, her nipples prominently displayed against the thin fabric. She wore no bra, and her breasts swayed up and down as she moved her body.

As women went, if Marina was going to engage in a little lesbian action, she'd definitely choose one as sensual as the willowy blonde.

Rora slid alongside Marina, slithering her body close, pressing her breasts against her as she wrapped her arms around Marina's waist. The music slowed as a new song began. A slow one, meant for couples. Rora twined her arms tighter around Marina and rested her fingertips along the small of Marina's back.

Having no choice but to reciprocate, Marina wound her arms around Rora's neck and allowed the woman to pull her in closer. Their hips met and Rora rocked against Marina's pelvis.

Heady stuff, indeed. She'd never realized she could be so turned on by another female. Maybe it was because they were in a public place and people watched. Marina fought back a snicker. First the restaurant, and now a crowded dance floor. She never knew she possessed the characteristics of an exhibitionist, but showing off like this was quite a turn on.

If nothing else, this assignment was sure as hell enlightening.

Rora's breasts were pliant, her scent like sweet gardenias, her lips full and painted a shiny pink. Marina fleetingly wondered what she'd taste like, having only experienced the flavor of her own juices before.

"Where's your Dom?" she asked Rora.

"He's over there."

Marina followed Rora's pointed finger. A tall, slender man in brown leather and a floor-length coat stood just off the dance floor, his intense gaze trained on them. He had shoulder-length, straight black hair, a long, hawkish nose, and the darkest eyes she'd ever seen. Incredibly sexy, he smiled in a self-satisfied way that led her to believe he had just gotten exactly what he wanted.

Wrong, bucko. What you got was to enjoy a little voyeurism. That was as far as she'd go with Rora.

She turned back to smile at her dance partner, then quickly grasped Rora's arms as a wave of dizziness threatened to send her to the floor.

"What's wrong, Marina?"

"Whoa," she said, shaking her head to clear the sudden fog. "Must be that drink. I might have downed it too quickly."

A concerned frown appeared on Rora's face. "You do look a little pale. How about some fresh air?"

She could barely stand as nausea overcame her and her legs wobbled. The desire to lie down in the middle of the dance floor was overwhelming. "Get me out of here," she gasped, grateful for Rora's arm slipping around her waist and guiding her off the floor.

Marina blinked and tried to see in front of her, but everything had gone blurry. She could barely make out the tall giant of a man in front of her.

"You don't look well, little one," he said. "Rora, let me take her."

"Yes, Sire."

She nearly lost it as she was swooped up into his arms. She fought to remain conscious, realizing that she'd been drugged.

By Rora? Her befuddled mind couldn't comprehend that the meek blonde would do that. Perhaps she was instructed to do so by her sire, the man who carried her against his rock-hard chest.

They walked through a door and were suddenly outside. It wasn't the front door. Some back or side entrance maybe? Dammit, she couldn't even lift her head. She didn't have the strength to fight. Hoping he was one of the kidnappers, she prayed she hadn't fallen into some other trap. One that she wouldn't be able to escape from.

Unable to fight the effects of whatever drug she'd been given, she closed her eyes and gave herself up to the blissful darkness.

* * * * *

Marina heard sounds, but her eyelids were heavy and she couldn't force them open. Her mouth was so dry it hurt and she was desperate for a drink.

Voices whispered nearby. She tried to move, but something prevented her from doing so. Dammit, she was so tired! She fought to remember what had happened before she woke, but her mind was a dense mass of...nothing. Where had she been before? And more importantly, where was she now? How long had she been unconscious?

Finally managing to pry her eyelids open, she fought past the drug-induced haze and looked around.

She was in a room. The walls were light in color. A harsh light shined overhead, but she didn't see the source of it. Sunlight maybe? No, she felt no heat on her body. In fact, she was downright chilled.

The voices were behind her, whispering. Two people at least, but she couldn't hear what they were saying. Cold, metal bindings surrounded her wrists and ankles. The table she laid on was uncovered and just as icy as the room temperature around her.

Now she remembered, at least parts of it. She was undercover, and she'd been to the BDSM club. But that's all she remembered.

Her teeth began to chatter and she started to shiver. Couldn't they have thrown a blanket over her? At least she was still dressed, although the outfit she'd worn to the club didn't afford her much in the way of warming coverage.

"What's wrong, dear lady? Are you cold?"

A deep voice resounded behind her. He appeared beside her, a giant of a man, his body so wide it cast a shadow over hers.

He looked human, except for a face covered with interesting looking tattoos. He was bald, the skin of his head pierced four times across the top as if they'd grabbed his skin and sewn it together with long needles, then left the needles in his scalp. The tattoos were all different colors and almost completely covered his face, head and neck. She'd seen her share of aliens on Earth, but never one that looked like him.

"I am Zim, slave master of Xarta."

Marina let out the breath she'd been holding, grateful that she'd at least made it to the right planet. Hell, she must have been out for a couple days to take a flight to this planet without waking. How odd. Even the high-speed travel rockets took a minimum of two Earth days to reach the Meloxian galaxy.

The fog finally clearing from her mind, she managed to open her eyes and cast Zim an angry, frightened look. "Where am I? How did I get here?"

"You are where you should be. How you got here is not for you to know. What you need to know I will tell you."

"Just wait a minute. Who the hell are you to—"

Her words were cut off by a lightning-like zing of electric shock that coursed through every muscle, making her nearly leap off the table despite her bindings. Shit, that hurt! She felt the lingering, unpleasant tingle at her neck. She was wearing some kind of collar.

Obviously an electrical one.

"You will not speak again unless spoken to. That was a mild correction. The next one will really be painful."

The bastard enjoyed inflicting pain, too. She could tell by his leering expression. She'd like to take whatever electrical shock device he'd just used on her and shove it up his ass. Nevertheless, she remained mute.

"You have been brought to Xarta to serve as a submissive to a dominant male. You will be taught how to behave, how to act as an obedient slave, and how to serve the sire who purchases you at auction tonight. You will shortly be taken to the preparation room where potential bidders can peruse those who will go out for sale this evening. At no time are you to speak unless you are directly asked a question. Is that understood?"

Tamping down the urge to tell him what she really thought, she nodded, wishing she could turn this into an out-of-body experience. Kaden had explained some of what might happen during preparation and auction, although she got the idea that he was being purposely vague. She didn't look forward to any of it.

A couple men with facial tattoos similar to Zim arrived shortly thereafter. They removed her shackles and dragged her into a standing position. Marina fought the sudden dizziness that threatened to drop her to her knees, grateful for their supporting strength.

They led her into another room. It was very warm in the room, and a large, sunken bath centered the chamber. Two women stood in the bath, completely naked and heads bowed. One was a pale creamy color, the other had a near lavender tinge to her skin. Both had three breasts!

On Earth she saw her share of alien cultures, but usually not naked ones. Interesting to see a third breast popping up between the other two.

Marina was quickly stripped by the two men and fought back the embarrassment of having to stand naked in front of them. They seemed oblivious to her discomfort as they led her toward the bath.

"Get in. Don't try to escape or struggle or you'll be punished."

Where would she go? The only way out was through two doorways, and the extremely tall men positioned themselves at each one to block her only escape. She only hoped her sizzling collar wouldn't electrify her when she entered the water.

She stepped into the bath, the warm, steaming water heating her chilled skin. Without speaking or looking at her, the women picked up square, rough, sponge-like objects. Actually they looked sharp and painful, but fortunately the scrubbing felt great. They began at her neck and washed her from top to bottom.

Oh, why not just enjoy it? She'd just think of this as one of those spa vacations where she was pampered and catered to.

After she'd been bathed and had her hair washed, the women led her from the tub and patted her dry with a warm towel. Left naked, she was taken once again by the men guarding her through yet another doorway.

This time, she dug in her heels as she realized she would not be alone in the next room.

There were other naked women in the room, all strapped to tables that tilted up and back. Most were straight up, their arms and legs shackled as Marina had been when she first woke. But that wasn't the worst part.

The outer wall was glass. On the other side of the glass stood a group of men, all watching with rapt interest.

"I don't think so," she mumbled, more to herself than to her guardians.

"Silence, woman!" They gripped her upper arms and dragged her to a table, quickly strapping her in and tilting her upward so she faced the glass wall.

There had to be two dozen men staring through the glass, all of their gazes suddenly fixed on her! Heat rose from her breasts to her neck, and she was grateful for her dark skin so that the embarrassed blush wouldn't show.

She'd never felt more exposed in her life.

One of the women in the room wept softly. Two of them looked like drugged zombies, their eyes glassy, empty, as if they'd had their souls ripped from them. One was Soreelian, with red dots over her body. Although the normal red dots had turned a pale pink as she stared lifelessly at the ceiling.

Soreelians were vivacious creatures, full of life and laughter. She'd never seen one so subdued, so frightened. The small woman's body trembled, and a red tear rolled down one cheek.

Bastards. What had they done to her? Soreelians were a peaceful race. They wouldn't know conflict, had no experience with it. To have one of their women taken against their will was unheard of. Their race died without freedom of choice.

This was why she was here and she needed to slap herself across the face with that harsh reminder. Her assignment wasn't about what she liked and didn't like. Her comfort didn't matter. She was here to free these women and prevent others from being imprisoned.

A female with bowed head approached with a wand-like device in her hand. Lord, she hoped it wasn't going to be another electrical zapping. When the woman waved the wand over her legs, she felt a warmth envelop her skin, but no pain.

"What are you doing?" she asked the woman.

The woman glanced over at one of the guards, who nodded. Without making eye contact with Marina, she said, "I am removing all your body hair."

Okay, that she could live with. The wand cast a warm glow within her, tingling slightly as the woman waved it over her pussy. Marina watched in rapt fascination as the hair on her sex completely disappeared. Soon, all her body hair had been removed.

She wished she had one of those devices on Earth. *This* was the way to remove body hair!

Of course, now she was more exposed than ever before, especially since the guards pulled her legs apart and refastened her bindings to the very edge of the table. When they tilted the table slightly backwards, her sex was pointing toward the glass wall.

She wanted to look away, didn't want to watch the men ogling her, but then she spotted a familiar male form in the center of the throng.

Kaden.

Her heart sped up at the sight of him. He was dressed in brown suede pants that laced at the crotch and a loose-fitting white shirt open halfway down, revealing his bronzed chest. Damn, he looked like one of those ancient cowboys of Earth, hard and muscled and dangerous as hell. Her mouth watered at the sight of him. His gaze was trained only on her, and even though he stood some distance away she saw the heat in his eyes, turning them a molten amber.

Relief washed over her and she suddenly felt safe again. And not so alone. Strange how someone she barely knew could make her feel so comforted, especially considering what was about to happen.

Then it occurred to her that he was seeing her completely naked. She wished her arms were free so she could cover herself, which was ridiculous since Kaden had already seen her sex, up close and personal at the restaurant. She might as well get over her embarrassment, because this wasn't going to get any easier.

Zim, the slave master she met earlier, approached with what looked to be some funky looking gun. It had a long barrel and a trigger, but the end of the barrel widened, and in between was some kind of shiny metal, curved into a U-shape.

Oh, this didn't look good. She squirmed, to no avail of course. Whatever it was he had in his hand, she wanted no part of it.

She watched him closely as he laid the barrel against her left nipple, very afraid that she wasn't going to like what was about to happen.

"What are you doing?"

"Silence!" He glared at her. "Relax, woman. This will not hurt."

Yeah, right. She'd heard that one before.

She tensed and he pulled the trigger.

Heat seared her breast. Not painful, it was like slipping into a very hot bath. Her breast warmed and her nipple tingled, then the sensation disappeared.

Glancing down at her breast, she saw that he had pierced her nipple with the curved metal. It was silver, shimmering against her dark areola. Zim performed the same task on her other nipple.

Finally letting out the breath she'd been holding, she relaxed a bit. Not that she cared a whole lot for this way of branding females. At least it hadn't been a form of torture.

She'd never been one for body adornment, but, admittedly, the dangling silver didn't look too bad.

"The Dom who purchases you at auction tonight will affix the jewels of his choosing to your nipples. And to your sex," he added, right before pressing the barrel to her clit and firing.

Marina stiffened as the heat washed over her, then calmed when it quickly dissipated. She assumed the same type of silver jewelry now adorned her clit.

"You will find these quite enjoyable, especially as a reward," Zim said, leaning over and caressing her cheek. She shuddered, revolted by his touch and the way he leered at her. "You need only act the obedient submissive and you will find many pleasures here in Xarta."

Uh-huh. Nothing appealing at all about becoming some man's slave, even if that man was Kaden. Reminding herself that she was here for a valid reason, she didn't respond to the slave master.

She'd save her act for the auction tonight, where she'd let them all know she wasn't about to become some man's play toy.

When Zim moved away, she caught sight of Kaden again. He stood in front of the glass wall with his arms crossed over his chest and a wicked smirk on his face. Her gaze traveled over his body and focused on the sizeable erection pressing against his pants. Her pussy flared and moistened, her mind awash with images of his long cock plunging inside her cunt.

He arched a brow and offered her a half smile. Hell, he knew what she was thinking, knew he affected her physically.

If he thought she'd be embarrassed by all this, he was wrong. She was doing her job and she always succeeded in her assignments. She would not take this personally, she would not get involved, and she would *not* continue to think the hot thoughts she'd been thinking about Kaden.

By the time this farce had reached its conclusion, she'd most likely feel nothing but loathing for him. He was, after all, an inherent Dom.

And she sure as hell was no man's submissive.

* * * * *

Kaden was mesmerized by the sight of Marina's pussy glistening in the harsh light of the viewing room. Beads of moisture glistened on the bronzed lips of her newly pierced cunt.

He remembered the sweet taste of her and his cock tightened against his pants.

Soon, very soon she'd be his to command. The thought enticed him, had been on his mind in the days since he'd last seen her.

His arrival on Xarta had been mixed with the welcome feeling of home and an alien-like experience. This place wasn't at all like he remembered, which shouldn't surprise him. One of the reasons he'd left the planet was the sweeping change in the way domination and submission was handled.

He'd never condoned slavery. There were too many women willing to become submissives for Xartanians to have to resort to kidnap and slavery. He'd thought it was an anomaly, something that wouldn't be tolerated on his home planet.

He'd been wrong. And because of it, he'd left. He'd like to say it was because he was indignant over the slavery issue, but frankly, he'd grown bored with submissives who were too eagerly willing to do his bidding. The women native to Xarta were genetically predisposed to become submissives. It was as it had been for centuries, and most Doms accepted it, reveled in it.

Kaden hadn't. He'd tried it for years, had relationships with many native Xartanian women, and yet had always felt unfulfilled. So he had never mated with a woman, and had yet to bring children into the world. It was possible he never would.

Maybe he was the anomaly, torn between the desire to take a woman and force her to submit to him and knowing that enslaving a woman against her will went against the old laws of Xarta, against his own personal laws.

At least the way Xarta used to be. Over the years, more and more of the dominant males had grown tired of the easily submissive females native to the planet. As a result, Xarta had been forced to change to meet the needs of its people. He still didn't like it, even if the desires of the dominant men on his planet mirrored his own. He accepted who he was, which didn't mean he had to act on it.

Except now. With Marina, he would fulfill one fantasy. To own a woman who didn't want to be dominated. But he'd have to walk a fine line between having what he most desired and remembering that he was on a mission. He and Marina were playing a game. This wasn't reality.

Heaving a sigh of frustration, he watched the way she looked at him, her chin held high as if daring him to try to control her. Her emerald eyes glittered bright against her copper skin. The piercings were a stark contrast of light silver against her dusky areolas. Her nipples beaded tight against the silver circlets, and he imagined running his tongue over their pebbled peaks.

This needed to happen soon. He hadn't come since before that night he'd pleasured her in the restaurant several days ago. His balls ached, filled with release he needed to spill deep inside her.

Once the women had been pierced, they were released and taken from the room. Kaden stepped into the auction room, keeping to the back so that he could monitor the other men in attendance.

He hadn't seen who had taken Marina from Earth and brought her here, but he assumed she knew. Once they had some time alone, he could question her. Other than reestablishing himself on this planet and putting out a search for a copper-skinned woman with light eyes, he hadn't made much headway into determining the identity of the slave traders.

Zim assured him the women who had been brought for auction were there willingly, that it was their secret desires to be enslaved and dominated. He told Kaden the women would object, but it was all for their own and their new sires' pleasure. He swore the women had all come to the planet of their own accord and signed the oath of free will upon their arrival in Xarta.

Kaden knew better, and soon Zim's reign as slave master would be over. First, the auction.

The auction floor was an oval-shaped, raised platform. Zim appeared, made his introductions and explained how the auction worked. There would be a minimum set bid for each female depending upon the amount of interest expressed during the showing.

The first three women were presented, bid upon and purchased. Arguments ensued over bids and winners. As was typical, women auctioned as slaves were quite sought after. He heard many disgruntled whispers throughout the crowd when someone lost out on a particular female.

Finally, it was Marina's turn and he stepped into the middle of the throng of eager men pushing their way up toward the platform.

His pulse pounded as she was led onto the stage, a submission collar attached around her neck. Dressed in a see-through gown the same emerald green as her eyes, the garment barely covered the sides of her breasts. A tasty view of the curve of her hips and thighs was visible on each side.

She looked like a golden seductress, her hair pulled away from her face, wild curls spilling over her shoulders and down her back. As she was led into the center of the stage, she pulled against the collar, wincing when Zim corrected her with the electrical shock.

Her eyes blazed green flames and Kaden was taken by her fire. She would not be easy to tame, yet his connection with her told him that she didn't yet know what she wanted. Inside the feisty beauty was a woman who needed a man to dominate her sexuality, to give her all that she sought and had never found before.

A strong woman needed a strong man to tame her, to pleasure her.

He was that man.

"We will begin the bidding at one thousand *parlons*," Zim said, smiling as the crowd hushed before him. "This one has a temper, and is a lush vixen unparalleled by others of her kind. She will be sold quickly, and will make quite a catch for a very strong Dom. Who will be the first to tame this beauty?"

Marina could have snorted at the way Zim described her. Lush, vixen, beauty. What a crock. She searched the crowd, finally spotting Kaden in the middle of the group of men bidding her price up frantically.

Yet Kaden hadn't yet raised his hand or spoken up. She sucked in her bottom lip, knowing he was just waiting for…well, waiting for something, obviously.

She didn't know how much a *parlon* was, but she was suddenly worth more than ten thousand of them. The men below her seemed as if in a frenzy, their lust-filled gazes raking over her nearly nude body. The thin gown she wore was nothing more than sheer fabric with a hole cut out for her head. She had a sash tied loosely around her waist, but her entire body was visible through the fabric, no doubt showcasing every one of her ample curves.

Were these guys blind? Why were they bidding so highly on her?

And why *wasn't* Kaden bidding on her at all? What if Zim abruptly ended the auction and she ended up sold to another Dom? She could fake this submission thing with Kaden because it was her job. But with someone else? Hell, she'd rather be dead than give up her freedoms.

What if she'd been set up? Could Kaden be involved in the slave ring? Had she been purposely entrapped into this, only to be sold and forever disappear within Xarta? Earth's treaty forbade interference on this planet. They'd never be able to recover her. She'd be doomed to spend her days as a slave.

No. She forced her rambling thoughts aside, searching again for Kaden within the crowd. Only he wasn't there. Panic thrust her heart against her chest, fear making her legs weak and trembling. The bids had slowed now, and Zim raised his hand as if to announce the winner.

"One hundred thousand *parlons*."

A collective gasp washed over the crowed at the amount offered, nearly three times as much as the last bid.

"Sold!" Zim's voice rang out over the crowded room.

She spotted him as he made his way through the parting crowd. Marina's eyes met the amber heat of her new sire.

Kaden now owned her.

Chapter Four

Zim's voice rang out loud enough for everyone in the room to hear. "This slave has been sold to Kaden!"

Marina watched Kaden approach the platform. He handed his payment card to Zim, then took the leash from the slave master's hands.

"Back away from my slave," he said. Zim bowed and moved quickly aside.

Kaden turned his gaze on her, a fire in his eyes like nothing she'd seen before. He swept her hair away from her ear and nuzzled her neck, whispering to her.

"This is for the audience. Fight me."

He pulled away, wound her hair around his fist and tugged it hard, forcing her head to tilt back. He kissed her, his mouth coming down over hers hard and furious, his tongue plunging within and ravaging hers. Fucking her mouth with his tongue, he drove it deep inside the recesses of her mouth as if it were a cock.

Marina couldn't breathe. Her thoughts had sailed away on the strength of Kaden's stunning kiss. Her nipples hardened, the tender buds scraping against his muscled chest. His free hand clenched her buttocks, pulling her against his erection. She gasped into his mouth, shocked at the moans that spilled from her lips.

Fight me. Lost in the delicious sensation of his stroking tongue, she'd momentarily forgotten his words. Of course she had to fight him. What was she doing?

She tore her mouth away from his, pushed hard against his chest and stepped back, wiping the back of her hand across her lips. Spitting at him, she said, "You will *never* own me!"

Kaden's eyes narrowed and he tugged the leash attached to her collar, driving his hand down so quickly that she fell to her knees. She looked up and shot him a venomous glare.

The crowd below them went wild as he arched a brow at her. Swallowing hard, she realized she was inches away from his hard cock, the scent of his aroused sex permeating her senses.

"Look down at the floor, woman. Dare not look up at me or I will demonstrate my mastery of you before this entire room."

She didn't doubt for a second that he'd do what he said. But she wasn't going to make it quite that easy for him. Her gaze lingered on his for more than a few seconds. Despite her fervent desire to tell him exactly what he could do with himself, she finally dropped her chin to her chest and stared at the floor.

Once again the crowds cheered.

Kaden left her on her knees while he carried on a conversation with Zim. With every passing second she grew more and more irritated at this humiliating treatment.

After the applause died down, Kaden pulled on the leash and drew her up, turning away and walking off the stage. She had no choice but to try and keep up with his long strides. Whistles and bawdy comments followed them as they left the auction room.

With every step down the long hallway, her anger mounted. She pushed away thoughts of his heated kiss, concentrating instead on the smug look he'd given her when he had her on her knees before him. He was damn lucky she didn't decide to take a bite out of him right then. Which certainly would have showed him that such a position did not put one in control.

He led her to a room at the center of a hall, sticking his fingers into a gooey-like substance that caused the wide doorway to slide open. As soon as she walked through behind him, the door shut, the sound like the prison doors on Earth closing.

Subtle light glowed from swirling, floating candles, their scent bathing the room in a perfume reminiscent of fresh lavender. The smell assaulted her senses and made her think of warmth and summer. A bed covered in soft, cream-colored satin centered the room, with several chairs, a chaise and some kind of contraption that looked like a folding table. Along the far wall was a long wardrobe with huge double doors. She'd bet it didn't contain extra blankets and pillows.

Soft, strange music unlike anything she'd ever heard before filled the room.

Kaden turned to her, running his fingers along the leather collar that was affixed to her neck. His breath was warm and sweetly scented by some kind of liquor. He leaned in and pressed his lips to her neck, licking the pulse point that pounded erratically.

"We are being watched," he whispered, his lips moving alongside her ear. "Do not say anything that would give us away."

When he moved back, the softness she heard in his voice was not reflected in his hard stare. "You will require much training to break you of your rebelliousness."

Despite the fact this was just an act, she couldn't help her elemental response to his statement. Lifting her chin, she met his glaring look. "I don't need any training. I want to go home."

"You *are* home. Forget where you came from, for you'll never return there again." Gripping her chin in his hand, he leaned in so that his breath brushed her cheek. "And never look me in the eyes unless I give you permission to do so. Lower your head and look at the ground."

"Kiss my—"she started, then sucked in a breath and fought off the pain as a searing jolt struck her nerve endings. Goddamit she hated that device. It reminded her of a fucking cattle prod. It wasn't as painful as it was surprising. What annoyed her the most was that she had no control over it. She made a mental note to use it on every man in this place before she left this planet. "—ass," she finished, unable to resist.

A quick zap, harder this time. Shit. Quickly, she lowered her head, staring down at his feet.

"Good start." He pulled her toward two chains dangling from the ceiling, pulling up her hands and fastening her wrists with the cuffs at the end of each chain. He pulled her legs apart and attached her ankles with two cuffs tethered to the floor. He disengaged the leash from her collar and stood in front of her.

"Watch me," he said, then began to undress.

Marina swallowed, though her throat had gone dry.

He pulled the shirt over his head and discarded it on the bed. His abdomen was sculpted, the muscles taut, his belly flat.

Wow. His skin wasn't as dark as her natural coloring, yet still a healthy bronze. His chest was smooth and rippled with muscles that contracted, making her want to run her fingers over his skin. A tattoo covered the upper left part of his chest. Some kind of planetary symbol, she supposed. It was a colorful circle with a teardrop in the center.

Suddenly anxious to view the secret he hid beneath his pants, her gaze remained fixated on the laces as he slowly undid one, another, yet another, then slid his hand past the down of golden hair just inside the leather waistband. He pulled the pants over his slender hips and down his muscular legs.

His cock was long and thick, surrounded by a nest of golden, curling hair. Another tattoo ran the length of his shaft, this time swirling patterns in solid green, resembling the cresting waves of the ocean.

He approached her slowly, then stopped right in front of her. "Look at me."

She looked up into his face. He seemed angry, a slight tic pulsing alongside his temple. "First, you will not speak unless I tell you. If I ask you a question, you are allowed to answer. You will address me as 'Sire' at all times. You will not use my given name unless I give you permission. Second, you will remain a respectable distance behind me when we are walking unless I direct you otherwise. Third, you will follow every one of my commands exactly as I give them to you, precisely at the moment I give them to you, or you will be punished."

Yeah, right. What could he do to her that hadn't already been done? In the past few hours she'd been stripped down, paraded naked in front of a horde of lascivious men and then forced to kneel before him like a…like a…slave. Which was exactly what she was supposed to be.

She bowed her head, keeping her mind occupied with thoughts of Kaden's painful demise.

"Tell me your name."

"Marina."

"Sire."

She grit her teeth and spit out the name. "Sire."

"A beautiful name, which matches the lovely woman."

She snorted, and he yanked her chin up and glared at her. "What was that sound?"

"Nothing."

"Sire." He followed it up this time with another zap. Goddamit!

"You don't think you're beautiful?"

How the hell was she supposed to answer that? No, she didn't think she was beautiful at all. "I'm okay…Sire."

"That we'll have to work on. You are more than just 'okay', Marina. Why do you think those men vied to purchase you out there tonight? Why do you think I bid so much on you? Because you're hideous?"

No, because they were working undercover and he had to, not because he wanted to. Would he have bid on her if she was a stranger to him? Doubtful. It was hard for her to believe that with all the hot bodies running around this place she would be in any demand whatsoever.

"I asked you a question."

"No, I don't think I'm hideous, Sire." Which she wasn't, so at least that was the truth. She wasn't beautiful, either.

"Good. Now let's get you out of that gown."

How was he going to do that when she was—

Oh. Ripped it to shreds. The flimsy garment made sense now. Easy to remove.

She was beginning to really hate this assignment. And it was getting worse with every passing second. Since he'd already seen her naked, there was no point in trying to hide her body.

"Look at me, Marina."

She did so, not quite believing the desire she saw in his eyes. He approached her, something clasped in his hand. She gasped when he opened his palm and spotted the most perfect emeralds she'd ever seen. Shock filled her as he fastened one teardrop-shaped stone to the piercing on each her nipple. A smaller, smooth round emerald remained.

"These stones are tuned to my energy and mine alone. I command them. When you feel their movement, it is because I wish it."

The emeralds danced along the curved silver, vibrating lightly. She shivered at the exquisite sensation.

Her breath stopped when he knelt before her pussy. She nearly jumped out of her skin when his knuckles brushed her sex as he fastened the smaller emerald at the piercing on her clit.

"Beautiful. You smell so sweet, too." His tongue snaked out and caressed the folds of her slit. She licked her lips and swallowed past the knot in her throat. Despite her resolve to feel nothing, his tongue was hot, moist and teasing her to a near orgasm after only a few strokes. She fought back the disappointment when he stood, refusing to let him see how he affected her.

The emerald tingled and warmed against her clit, and she struggled to pay attention.

Kaden released the tension on the chains, allowing enough slack to push her forward into a bent over position.

He could barely contain his lust as he viewed Marina's delectable rear end in her face-down position. She had a magnificent ass—bronzed, firm and lush. The kind a man could grab onto and squeeze while he sank within her heated cunt.

His first thought was to plunge between the twin globes and sink into her tight back entrance. But he held back, knowing they would both reach a higher pleasure the longer he waited.

First, he had to teach her that as a submissive she had no control. Soon enough she would learn that she could receive great delights by simply obeying his commands.

Although the truth was, he enjoyed the spitfire within her. Marina was a natural sexual being, simmering with heated passion that he knew no man had yet explored. A restrained sensuality lurked beneath her cool exterior, and he meant to delve deep inside her secret thoughts and desires until he forced it out of her.

He began by running his palms over her skin, starting with her feet. Her calves and thighs were firm and supple, the skin like the softest silk in the galaxies. The muscles underneath her skin tightened and trembled as he made his way along her body.

"Relax, Marina. I will tell you every step of the way exactly what I'm going to do to you."

He caressed her buttocks, smiling as she tightened at first, then relaxed when he began to gently knead the muscles. As soon as she was pliant, he smacked one of her cheeks with his hand. She tensed and squealed, more from surprise, he imagined, since he hadn't spanked her hard at all.

"Don't make a sound or I'll put a gag in your mouth."

She hissed, but made no further noises. Kaden continued to caress her buttocks, occasionally slapping them gently. Marina grew accustomed to his actions and was soon lifting her rear in anticipation of the spankings. His balls drew tight against his body. Touching her was so intensely pleasurable, more so than he'd ever imagined it would be. Her body was perfectly made for him. Not as skinny as so many of the Xartanian women. He wanted some flesh to touch, to squeeze, to sink his cock into a woman who had some substance. After all, how could he pleasure a woman who could break so easily? Marina had a very tough exterior, though underneath he sensed a frightened, insecure woman just waiting for the right man to dominate her, to show her pleasures she had only dreamed of.

He would give her all that she needed, and more. His pleasure would be her pleasure. She had yet to understand that, but she would soon enough.

"One of the things you will need to understand about a Dom and sub relationship is that you are not here to be humiliated or abused. There will be no torture, unless it's pleasurable to both of us. I will care for you, Marina, and when I take my pleasure from you, it will give you pleasure in kind."

The skin of her buttocks had turned red, his palm prints clearly visible after several minutes of carefully applied swats. When he walked behind her, he noticed the moisture glistening along her sex.

Marina had become aroused by the spanking, as he knew she would.

"For example, when I spank you, your cunt gets wet, doesn't it?"

She hesitated before answering with a quiet, "Yes."

He spanked her hard. "Yes, Sire."

She whimpered. "Yes…Sire."

"It pleases me to lay my hand upon your sweet ass. I love the feel of your skin. It makes me hard, makes me want to fuck you. But it also pleasures you to feel the sting against your buttocks, doesn't it?"

Again a small hesitation before answering, as if she fought telling him how she felt. "Yes."

He raised his hand to swat her again, but before his hand came down, she spoke.

"Sire."

He didn't spank her, although he wondered if she deliberately disobeyed him because she enjoyed his hand swatting her ass. "Our relationship will be built upon trust. I trust you will follow my commands, and you trust that I will satisfy you in every way possible."

When his hand connected with her ass cheeks again, this time a little harder, she shuddered, but not in pain. The scent of her desire filled the room, mixing with the sweet smell of the candles. It was truly intoxicating, and made waiting to thrust inside her even more difficult than he imagined.

With a smile, Kaden reached into the drawer underneath the table, pulling forth an object he knew would enhance her senses.

He laid his hand on the cleft between her reddened ass cheeks, but this time he caressed the hot flesh, slowly sliding his fingers along the line between her buttocks. He caressed her moistened sex, rewarded with her sharp inhalation.

She was behaving. Other than her hard breathing, she hadn't spoken. Her acquiescence pleased him. He supposed because it seemed she wanted the same thing he did. He hadn't hurt her, would never hurt her, so she had to realize she had nothing to fear from him.

"I'm going to put something inside your ass, Marina. You will enjoy this. The object starts out very small and thin. Then as your body grows accustomed to having the object inside you, it will expand to fit your contours, relying on my psychic commands to bring you the utmost enjoyment."

First he would make sure she was sufficiently lubricated, doing so by petting her slit until she quivered under his questing fingers. More and more of her sweet nectar released. He used the moisture to lubricate her puckered hole, then slowly slid the object past her sphincter muscles, easing it in gently while her body grew accustomed to the invasion. The plug was thin, so would not cause Marina any distress.

Later, it would expand to fit her. If he guessed correctly, she'd enjoy this game of punishment and reward.

The only sound in the room was her panting breath as he slid the plug deeper inside her. He used his other hand to caress her clit, making sure she remained moist and aroused. When he had slipped it all the way inside her with only the wide, jelly-like platform remaining, he stepped in front of her.

"Marina, I give you permission to speak. I want honest answers to my questions. Are you prepared to do that?"

"Yes...Sire."

He smiled, sensing her difficulty in adding that word when she addressed him. "Good. Do you like having the probe inside your ass?"

"Yes, Sire." The word quivered as it left her throat.

"Have you ever been fucked in the ass?"

"No, Sire, I haven't."

"Have you ever fucked yourself in the ass with a toy?"

"Yes, Sire."

Kaden grinned. A hot, sexual being who had never been with a man strong enough to give her what she needed.

He stroked her skin as he moved alongside her, gently massaging the small of her back, testing her muscles to be sure she wasn't uncomfortable. He wanted her aware of the subservience of the position, but his plan wasn't to torture her. Trailing his fingers along the sides of her breasts, he smiled when she shivered.

"Are you comfortable?"

"Yes, Sire."

He sent mental impulses to the emerald stones. She moaned in response to the tiny vibrations.

"Do you like that?"

"Yes, Sire."

"Do you want more?"

"Oh, yes, Sire."

"Good. Because I'm going to give you more than you ever thought possible, Marina. Starting right now."

Chapter Five

A part of Marina hated that Kaden had turned her into a puddle of arousal. The part of her that was strong, dominant, capable of taking care of her own sexual needs, railed against being so obviously at his mercy. At the same time, this was an incredibly new and amazing experience, letting a man control her pleasure.

And what pleasure it was. Whatever he'd slid into her ass was warming, vibrating and expanding. She'd never felt anything so incredibly arousing before. The spanking he'd rendered had only served to heighten her senses. The sharp, stinging pain had caused her pussy to throb expectantly.

Now if he'd just fuck her with that magnificent cock, she'd be in heaven. He seemed to know exactly where to touch her, and for how long, taking her to the point of orgasm and stopping just short. It was maddening. Hell, she'd behave herself if he'd just let her come.

On Earth she'd be demanding right now, telling him exactly what she wanted, what she needed. Not being able to speak drove her crazy.

Then again, she hadn't had to instruct him where to touch her, how to touch her, or what would bring her to the brink of orgasm. Kaden had known how without her having to utter a word.

His hands moved over her, stroking her hair, teasing her lips with his fingertips, running his palms over her back and buttocks. Occasionally he'd swat her ass with his palm, the action causing the vibrating plug in her ass to heat and expand. It even had begun to move as if he was physically pulling it out and sliding it back in. Which couldn't be, since both his hands were occupied on other parts of her body.

He seemed to be in no hurry, leisurely exploring every part of her, alternately stroking gently and using a stinging slap on her buttocks. It was enough to drive her to the brink of insanity, or at the very least the brink of what would no doubt be an amazing orgasm. If he'd only let it happen.

"Kaden, I need to come."

He stopped, and the plug in her anus began to retract.

"Didn't I tell you not to speak unless you were asked to do so? Did I not direct you to call me Sire?"

"Yes, but—"

She heard the door slide open, then close.

Where the hell had he gone? And how could he leave her in this position? Her pussy quaked, hovering on the edge of orgasm. But the emeralds had ceased vibrating, the anal plug had deflated, and she couldn't touch herself.

Dammit! She had no control here!

She waited for him to return. And waited. And waited some more.

It seemed like hours. Then again it could have been minutes. She straightened, her back stiffening from being bent over. The cuffs rubbed against her skin, irritating as hell. And the damn butt plug was still inside her. Although it wasn't doing her any good. She was still a throbbing mess of arousal with no way to climax.

Was Kaden ever coming back? How could he have left her at such a critical moment?

Panic began to set in. What if something happened to him? What if he was forced to give her up? Then what? She'd die before *really* submitting to a man.

Suddenly the door slipped open and she let out a breath as Kaden strolled in.

"Drop your gaze to the ground."

Without thinking, she did as he asked.

"You're being punished, Marina. Keep this in mind the next time you break the rules. You do not speak without permission. And you will come only when *I* say. If you ask to come, I will punish you. If you come without my permission, I will punish you harder next time."

Fury boiled within her. She wanted to scream at him, to fling curse after curse at him, then drop a well-timed kick to his balls and watch him writhe on the ground.

She hated having no control. Hated it, hated it, hated it!

"Bend over."

She complied, but she was well past any thought of desire for sex. Gritting her teeth, she was bound and determined to resist his touch. He'd get no pleasure from her today.

He laid his hands on her again, his touch soft, kneading the muscles that had grown tired. When he pushed a long, arched table in front of her so that she could rest her back muscles, then lengthened the chains so her arms weren't above her head, she refused to think of it as an act of kindness.

She refused to acknowledge the arousal that once again grew within her as he leisurely explored her body. That wasn't a quiver of excitement when he caressed her slit, nor was that her moaning when he slipped two fingers inside her pussy.

"You're wet."

No point in acknowledging that statement as it was quite obvious from the cream dripping down her thighs.

Damn him!

And the butt plug had started to grow and vibrate within her again.

"Remember, Marina, don't speak unless I give you permission. I'd hate to take you to the brink again, only to stop and leave you wanting."

Long past the point of irritation at his threats, she took them more as sensual promise now, a wondering of what would come next. Would he fuck her now? Would he lean over and press that hard body of his against hers, thrust his cock deep into her throbbing pussy and end the torment?

"Look up at me, Marina."

He walked to the chair across from this contraption she was lying over and sat in a cushioned chair, spreading his legs and watching her. With every rake of his heated gaze over her body, the object in her ass warmed, vibrated and moved within her. Marina couldn't hold back the whimpers of need any longer.

She met his gaze head on, knowing she couldn't say the words, but offering pleading thoughts. *Please, I need to come.*

His only response was an enigmatic smile. His gaze roamed over her, and in response, the dangling emerald at her clit sent vibrating impulses, causing her legs to tense as she rode out the delicious sensations. At any moment she knew she'd climax, yet every time she was right there, the vibrations ended, the pseudo-cock inside her ass deflating a bit.

This was the most frustrating experience of her life. And Kaden was causing it.

At least he appeared tortured as well. His cock stood rigid, the colorful tattooed waves clearly visible along his engorged shaft. Was he just going to sit there and stare at her, tormenting them both? Every nerve ending in her body screamed for completion.

"Tell me what you want, Marina."

"I need to come, Sire." She hated spitting that word out, but right now she'd do anything.

One corner of his mouth curved, showing that dimple. "I love it when you beg for me, Marina. I'll have to make you do it more often. Your voice has a raspy quality to it that I can feel inside me."

Then do something! Touch me, lick me, fuck me. Make me come, dammit!

Of course, he hadn't heard her mental pleas. Instead, he palmed his shaft and stroked it from base to tip, only exasperating her further. Marina licked her now dry lips, desperately thirsty for a taste of him. Hell, she could probably come from sucking his dick. But he didn't move, instead kept his gaze locked on hers as he circled the dark head with his thumb. Moisture glistened on the tip and he used that to lubricate his fingers.

When he spread his legs wider, his balls were visible. Tight, hard, and she knew they'd be hot. She pumped her ass up and down on the table, envisioning that hard cock buried deep inside her, so deep his balls would smack her clit, sending her right over the edge.

She wouldn't beg him to fuck her. It hadn't taken her long to learn this game and she knew that, at least in this, she could not win. At his mercy whether she liked it or not, she had to play along.

After a few minutes of watching Kaden thrust his cock through his enclosed hand, she began to move against the cushioned table, rubbing her swollen clit against the slick surface.

"Don't come Marina," he warned. "You really don't want to go through this kind of torment again, do you? I can guarantee, next time it will last much longer, and won't be nearly as pleasurable."

Goddamit! What did a girl have to do to get an orgasm around here?

As Kaden's hand movements increased, she forgot all about seeking her own pleasure. Transfixed on watching the way his jaw tightened, the muscles of his upper arm corded and bunched with the effort of his quick strokes. With his free hand he reached down and grabbed his balls, massaging them gently. The scent of his sex permeated the air around her and only heightened her already turbulent arousal.

She wanted to beg him to fuck her, to let her suck the cream from his cock, or to feel the heat of his liquid desire as he came all over her buttocks. She wanted him close to her when he came, not so far away, not where she couldn't feel him, taste him, experience the pleasure he'd denied her so far.

Sweat beaded on his upper chest as he thrust his hips up, propelling the shaft inside his tightly clenched fist. His nipples were hard knots and Marina could almost feel them between her lips. Would he come harder if she sucked his nipples?

There were so many things she wanted to ask him to do, to beg him to do, and yet she remained mute, watching this erotic show he put on for her, unable to do anything but lie there and wish it were any other way but this.

Finally, he stood and approached her, never once halting the rhythm of his stroking hand. The shaft inside her ass began to swell, the emerald charms hummed. Kaden stopped at her head, lifting her chin and bending toward her, pressing a soft kiss to her lips. She drank from his mouth greedily, hungry for his touch, his taste.

"Where do you want it?" he asked, his voice strained.

"Let me taste you, Sire" she said, knowing she'd make it good for him. She didn't understand this need to give him pleasure when he'd so determinedly denied hers, yet she wanted his orgasm almost more than she wanted her own.

"Open your mouth, Marina," he whispered. "I want to watch my come spurt into your mouth."

She squeezed her buttocks as the plug inside her swelled and vibrated.

"But you can't come. Do you understand, Marina? You do not have my permission to come."

Past the point of caring, she nodded and opened her mouth, presenting him with her tongue.

He leaned in and rested his free hand on her back, then grasped his shaft and pumped hard and fast. Marina inhaled the crisp scent of his desire, reaching out with her tongue and capturing the drops of fluid beading on the tip of his cock.

Kaden groaned and for the first time since this began, Marina felt like she controlled the situation. Even tied up and unable to move or give herself an orgasm, she had the control right now. Kaden's pleasure was up to her. She lapped furiously at the head of his cock, rewarded when the first spurt of his orgasm shot onto her waiting tongue.

Focusing her gaze on Kaden, she watched him scrunch up his face and open his mouth, letting out a roar as a hot spray of white come shot into her waiting mouth. She licked and swallowed as his climax rushed through him, taking in every drop of his flavor until there was nothing left to give.

The room went silent with the exception of Kaden's panting breaths. Sweat poured from his body, the drops spilling onto her back. When he recovered enough to move, he released her bonds, removed the plug from her ass, and gently pulled her upright.

Her legs wobbled and if he hadn't been holding onto her, she'd have fallen. Her nipples stood out like sharp points, her pussy throbbing with an ache that seemed to grow in intensity with every passing second.

Now, surely, it was her turn.

Releasing the chains holding her, he drew her to the center of the room and pulled her close, kissing her in a way that made her tremble all over. His mastery over her body was an amazing thing to her. No man knew her as well as Kaden did. And he really didn't know her at all.

His eyes were dark pools of amber, his mouth firmly set. A slight tic danced alongside the dimple next to his lips. Tension emanated from him and she knew exactly how she felt.

He waited. He wanted. What she could give him. His erection brushed her sex, sending sparks of furious arousal coursing through her.

"Touch me."

Until he uttered the words, she hadn't realized she'd been waiting for his command. She reached for his shaft, twining her fingers around its steely length. Velvet strength greeted her, his cock pulsing against the palm of her hand. She squeezed and drew her hand along the rigid contours, sliding her thumb over the soft head. A drop of clear fluid spilled from the tip and she swiped it away with her finger, drawing his sweet taste into her mouth.

"Suck it."

The words alone caused her to shiver. The thought of doing to him what he'd done to her in the restaurant had her licking her lips in eager anticipation. She had received his climax a few moments before, but she hadn't been the one to give it to him.

Dropping to her knees, she took his shaft in her hand, drawing the tip near her mouth. Her tongue snaked out and captured the drops of fluid gathering at the head of his cock, welcoming his flavor. He quivered as she licked the velvety top of his shaft, then placed her lips over him and lightly suckled.

"*Zejehr, min letonsay sool da fahl!*" he muttered. Marina had no idea what it meant, but he said the words so passionately, ending them on a stuttered groan. They must mean he enjoyed her mouth on him. Perhaps she'd ask him to teach her some of his Xartanian language. It had a lyrical, sensual sound to it, almost like Earth's French.

"Let me feel your teeth along the shaft," he commanded. "Lightly."

She shuddered at his sensual order, then complied by grazing the sides of his member. Kaden threaded his hands in her hair and pulled her closer to him.

"Yes, *zejehr*, like that. Now suck, hard and fast."

His words were like a caress over her body, driving her mad with the desire to knock him to the floor and climb on top of him. A fierce need to fuck him furiously drove her to take him as deeply as she could.

"Deeper."

How could she take him deeper? There was so much to his length, yet her mouth was so full of him she couldn't speak. He held her head and fucked her mouth, taking his shaft nearly all the way out before plunging once again between her lips.

Arousal beat against her vibrating nipples and sex. She reached one hand down between her legs, only to find that hand jerked away as Kaden bent over and removed it.

"You will not come until I tell you."

Sucking in a breath that rattled with both irritation and a powerful need to climax, she took his shaft in both hands, moving her fingers up and down the length of him while taking the head into the deep recesses of her throat.

She was poised at the brink of an orgasm, and could easily have one without touching herself. Yet Kaden's warning remained prominent in her mind. Not wanting to lose the delicious sensations coursing through her, she concentrated instead on drawing his release from his straining cock.

Freeing one hand from his shaft, she searched underneath for the twin sacs, massaging the ridge between them before cupping the globes in her hands and gently squeezing.

His balls contracted tight and hard, his sweet release erupted inside her mouth and he let out a guttural cry in his alien tongue. She milked his balls and swallowed his essence as he continued to hold her mouth captive with his thrusting member.

When there were only a few remaining drops of the tangy fluid, he withdrew, his cock still hard despite the copious amounts of come he had shot down her throat.

He tasted like sweet fruit.

Marina sat back on her heels, her body desperate for release, and wondered what game they would play next.

Surely he would tire of her after the minimal amount of dominance he would have to show to whomever it was that watched.

Watched. Someone had watched her give Kaden a blow job. No doubt still watched as he reached for her hands and drew her up, then tilted her chin up, forcing her to meet his gaze.

"You did well, Marina."

She didn't speak, not sure what the appropriate protocol was in this type of situation, and definitely not wanting another shock to mar the warm, wet desire between her legs.

"I smell your nectar. You were aroused sucking my cock?"

"Yes, Sire."

"Good. You have a very talented mouth." He traced the outline of her lips with his fingertip, then leaned in and kissed her, licking her tongue where the taste of him still lingered. She shivered and reached for him, desperate for the feel of his skin, his muscled strength against hers.

"But you have much to learn about pleasing me. And I think there's still a little too much fight in you. We'll have to break you of that."

He wasn't going to let her come. Goddamit, he was going to deny her what she needed the most right now. And he said he wouldn't torture her?

Bullshit. This was the worst form of torture imaginable.

And she was tired. Tired, yet coiled with need.

Exhaustion finally claimed her and she rested her head against his chest. She wasn't certain she could endure another punishment, and yet she knew she had no control over whatever he decided to do to her next.

Why in hell had she agreed to this? Frustration ate at her, the desire to scream and cry almost unbearable. Would he tie her up again, leave her wanting while he left her? Worse, was she going to have to endure pent-up arousal for her entire stay?

Maybe he'd never let her come. Maybe that was part of what they did here.

Hell, no wonder the women served their Doms so willingly. She'd do anything right now for an orgasm. Just one sweet, stress-relieving orgasm.

Instead, she just knew more torture was forthcoming.

She was surprised when he led her to the bed and laid her gently upon it, pulling the light sheet over her. He swept her hair away from her face and smiled down at her.

"Rest, *zejehr*. You've had a long day."

She wanted to ask him questions, like the meaning of the word he used frequently when speaking to her, what would happen next, and when she'd be allowed to come. She wanted to get her mind around finding the kidnapped women and finishing this mission, although admittedly that part had somehow been shoved to the back of her mind.

Tomorrow. She'd store all her questions inside her head until then. Kaden waved his hand over the wall panel and the lights dimmed. The day had been long and filled with stress and tension. Maybe they'd drugged her to get her to Xarta, because her limbs felt heavy and she had a hard time keeping her eyes open. No longer able to fight how tired she was, she closed her eyes, her mind awash with the monumental changes that had occurred in her life today.

Shut it down, Marina. Rest. You'll need your strength for what's coming.

For now, sleep was more important. Tomorrow, there'd be plenty to deal with.

Chapter Six

Kaden stood over Marina, watching her slumber. Light filtered in through the clear skylights above, casting a glow on her skin. She looked like a golden goddess, her dark skin glimmering in the sunlight, her hair cascading in wild curls over her shoulders and down her back. The sheet rode low on her hips, revealing the crest of her buttocks. She was magnificent.

And surprising.

He'd expected her to do her job. Laren had assured him of that. What he hadn't expected was the passionate response she'd given him last night. What he gave, she took. When he expected her to break, to give up, to scream at him, she hadn't. Instead, she'd flamed his senses, heightened his arousal, and damn near killed him with her luscious mouth. That, he hadn't expected.

If she was acting the part, she was giving an award-winning performance. He had guessed that she might be a submissive underneath her dominating, controlling exterior, but he had no idea that she'd adapt so readily to the pleasures he could offer. Even in punishment she had controlled his desire. He wasn't sure who was mastering whom here, because he was under her spell and wanted her more than he should.

As it was he had barely slept last night. Not that he needed to, but a fierce desire to crawl next to her on the bed and wrap her in his arms had been almost more than he could handle. He'd ended up leaving the room and scouting the palace for the women they sought.

He hadn't yet had an opportunity to ask Marina about her kidnapping. He'd been so absorbed with her as his sub that he hadn't taken her to a place where they weren't monitored.

It would have looked too suspicious anyway. He'd take care of the questioning this morning.

No luck yet, but perhaps later today at the meal they would share with all the palace citizens. If the women were still here, and last he heard at least some of them were, then he and Marina would be able to spot them. Last night he'd formed a plan. Today, he'd discuss it with Marina, if he could manage some private time with her. Too many of the rooms were monitored both visually and aurally.

Marina stirred and rolled over onto her back, the sheet slipping down to her waist. Her breasts glowed in the sunlight, the emeralds sparkling as they kissed the soft flesh of her nipples. He ached to cover her with his body, nuzzle the charms with his tongue before taking the peaks deep into his mouth and suckling her.

He undressed, wondering what she'd do if she woke and found him peeling off his clothes, his cock already semi-hard. Last night had been difficult, but necessary for her to learn the ways of a submissive. But he'd wanted her to come, wanted to feel her bucking underneath him, her sweet cunt squeezing the life force from him.

Instead, he'd taken her to the brink again and again, and then put her to bed to sleep.

Undressed, he approached the bed and leaned over, content for the moment to just watch her. She frowned in her sleep. A bad dream perhaps? He hoped not. Tiny creases appeared near her eyes when she scrunched her features like that. He wanted to taste her, touch her, hold her in his arms until she woke, then make love to her over and over again.

His cock twitched, stirring and ready for more. He'd yet to drive his shaft into Marina's sweet cunt and wasn't sure how much longer he could hold back. But here in Xarta, it was necessary to have her complete cooperation first. Once he was assured of complete dominance over her, then they would share their bodies.

She didn't yet understand what that meant, didn't realize that she would lose nothing of herself by giving her sexuality to his control. She would learn, though, and when she did, it would be the sweetest gift imaginable.

He smiled down at her, wondering if she was still aroused. He pulled the sheet back and grinned. Her hand rested on her slit, gently stroking her bare pussy even in her sleep.

Guess that answered his question. Her scent filled the room, vanilla and musky, making him desperate for a taste of her. How easy it would be to slip between her legs and lick the moisture beading there.

"Marina, wake up."

She groaned and lifted her hips, leisurely circling her clit with her fingers. His balls tightened.

"Now Marina. Wake up."

Her eyes opened partway, enough to glimpse the magic of her emerald gaze, as vibrant as the stones on her nipples. She smiled at him, then sat up, keeping her gaze focused at his feet as she slipped off the bed and stepped toward him.

Was she actually taking a submissive position with him? Or was she still too sleepy to acknowledge he was even in the room?

"Look at me."

She lifted her chin and met his gaze. Galaxies, she was lovely in the morning. Her skin flushed with sleep and warmth, her hair in wild disarray around her face, and her eyes still holding onto whatever dream had made her reach for her sweet pussy.

"Good morning, Marina."

"Good morning…Sire."

Kaden couldn't help his smile. "Very good. Come, we have much to do today."

He directed her into a privacy chamber where she could have a few minutes to herself. When she came out, he led her through a panel in the wall into the bathing room.

Marina's eyes widened as he led her into one of his favorite places on the palace grounds. A tropical oasis, the bathing room was actually located outside in a courtyard, surrounded by the pale coral walls of the rounded palace interior. This was one of the places where he and Marina could speak without being heard, especially this early in the day before the crowds came to bathe and play.

"This is lovely," she said in a hushed voice, then quickly turned to him as if in apology.

"It's okay. In this instance I won't punish you for speaking your thoughts. Be mindful of that fact in the future, though."

"Yes, Sire."

"Tell me what you remember of the kidnapping."

"Nothing. My mind is a blank from the time I entered the BDSM club until I woke up here."

"Interesting. Let me do some checking into that."

She nodded, barely listening to him as she took in the sights and sounds of the pool area.

An inexplicable satisfaction filled him as he watched her admiration of the things he also found enjoyable. It had never mattered before whether a submissive liked her surroundings or not. Then again, Kaden had a wary sensation of caring what Marina thought. His heart had never been part of relationships in the past. Whether he held that part of himself back or whether he hadn't found the right woman who struck a chord deep inside him, he didn't know. Something about Marina called to him, the depths of him, more so than any other woman he'd known before.

The feeling was unnerving.

Marina felt like she'd just entered a forest. Dense, overhanging trees similar to palms waved in the warm breeze. Instead of coconuts, though, purple oval fruit hung from each end of the fronds. The melodic songs of birds filled the thick, humid air. She looked up and saw colorful creatures not at all like birds. Sitting on the thick branches of the trees, they were fat like koalas and covered with green and red fur.

She inhaled and tropical scents greeted her, sweet, pungent and earthy.

Dark rocks of varying sizes surrounded a pool of water as blue as anything she'd ever seen. A light vapor of steam rose from the surface, making the air so thick she felt she could reach out a grab it with her hands. Running water fell over the rocks and into the pool, the rippling sound peaceful and calming.

"Sit here," Kaden commanded, motioning her to a small table and two thickly padded lounging chairs. She slipped onto one of them and he handed her a drink. It was orange, thick, and ice cold.

Marina wondered whether she still had permission to speak. After yesterday, the last thing she wanted was to be stretched out on that rack and tortured to near orgasm again. Last night she'd dreamed of nothing but sex. Her and Kaden and hours and hours of sensual pleasures. Somewhere in the back of her mind she remembered she had a job to do here, but also knew that Kaden would take the lead. Fighting him would do no good. Not on this planet, anyway. And if she could perform this mission and enjoy some amazing sex at the same time, why not? It's not like there was any permanence attached to their relationship.

When the mission was over, they were over. Simple and straightforward with no entanglements, just the way she liked it.

Right now she had to concentrate on his expectations so that she could avoid more of his wickedly sensual torture. Her body had still ached with arousal when she woke, and dammit she'd get an orgasm today even if she had to beg him for it.

She'd play the part to the extent she was capable, but she'd never give herself completely to him. Control was important. That she'd never truly give him.

His power over her required he manipulate her to his will. Two could play that game, and she'd bet he'd never realize what she was doing.

As she sipped the liquid, she surreptitiously glanced in Kaden's direction. He sipped his drink and stared at the water spilling into the pool. In profile, he was magnificent. Hell, in everything he was magnificent. Unashamed of his nudity, he reclined on the chair like he was posing for an artist. One foot flat on the lounge, knee bent, resting his arm on top of it. His cock, even when at rest, enticed her, making her mouth water for another taste of him.

She hadn't met many men like Kaden before. Okay, admittedly, she'd never met *anyone* like him. The men she knew were all strong on the outside, for certain. The ones she'd slept with had no clue what women wanted.

That is, they'd had no clue what *she* wanted. She was in charge of enough in her daily life. Just once she wanted to have a man who knew exactly what he needed, with enough insight to also know what she needed.

Oh hell, Marina. Make up your damn mind! Do you want control over every aspect of your life, including sex? Where has that gotten you? Nothing. No orgasm, no satisfaction. Never.

Why couldn't she submit to Kaden willingly? Was it so difficult to let someone else take charge of her pleasure?

And why not give it up to someone who clearly knew her body almost as well as she did.

She quickly averted her gaze when Kaden glanced over in her direction.

"You don't have to remain silent. We're alone for the time being and not being monitored. Just remember to take the position of submission should someone walk in."

She nodded, feeling oddly uncomfortable. How was she supposed to get used to acting like a submissive slave if they had to pop in and out of their roles all the time? "If you don't mind, I'd like to continue the act, even if we're talking about the case. Makes it easier that way and I won't forget to do as I'm supposed to."

He arched a brow and nodded. "Or perhaps you enjoy the role more than you're admitting?"

Not a chance. She looked away, staring out over the pristine water of the pool. "I'm just doing my job, Kaden."

His silence forced her attention back to him. He nodded, his facial expression revealing nothing of his emotions. "Of course you are."

Wasn't she? She hadn't known Kaden that long, and besides, she never developed emotional attachments to the men she fucked. She merely fucked and forgot them.

The allure of Kaden was that he hadn't allowed the fucking part to commence, and she was more than ready for it. What was wrong with him, anyway? She thought a Dom would be screwing her ten different ways in the first hour. As it was, they'd spent two evenings together, and not once had she felt his cock inside her pussy.

Kind of annoying, now that she thought about it.

"I went scouting for the women last night," he said.

She turned to him, grateful to have something else to think about. "And?"

Shrugging his shoulders, he said, "Nothing. No sign of them, at least not in any of the public areas of the voyeur rooms."

"That's not good. Are you sure they're here?"

"Yes. We'll be taking a meal with the rest of the palace today. We can look for them then. I have a plan that, when we find them, may work to get us alone with the women to talk."

"And would that plan consist of you fucking any of those women?"

His eyes darkened. "Do you have some problem with that?"

Now it was her turn to shrug. "Of course not. One fuck is just as good as another." So much for thinking there was something different about Kaden. She wasn't about to let him know she might have any feelings for him. He already had enough of an advantage over her.

Besides, she had no right to get jealous and possessive of Kaden. He wasn't hers, any more than she was his.

"Oh, I don't know about that. Maybe in your culture that's true. It's different with Xartanian Doms and their subs."

"Different? In what way?"

He smiled. "Those who don't live the kind of lives we do simply don't understand. There's an emotional bonding when a dominant and a submissive become one. It isn't just physical, or even the mental aspect of dominating another."

"What is it then?"

He pointed to his heart, below the tattoo. "It comes from within. A sharing, a merging of wants and needs. For example, if you were a true submissive, I'd be able to give you what you needed, and you'd do the same for me."

She frowned. "In other words, I can't satisfy your needs because I'm not a true submissive."

His lips curled upward in a smile that made her stomach flutter. "Not necessarily. You were doing fine last night."

Heat crept into her skin and she forced her gaze away from his eyes. "Is that why you left before? Because keeping slaves didn't meet your needs?"

"Partly. Just like your people on Earth, everyone on Xarta is unique. Some prefer the born submissives, while others prefer women who put up more of a struggle. That's why they started bringing in females from other planets. More fight in them. But no, I have no desire to own a woman completely unwilling to submit to me. I have no desire to completely break someone. There is no pleasure in that kind of situation. Not for me, anyway."

"Then you must prefer the women who are naturally submissive."

"Not really."

And they said women were confusing? "I don't understand. Xartanian women are born submissives. Why couldn't they meet your needs?"

He stood and roamed the room, pulling one of the oval fruit from a tree and peeling its top layer away. "I don't really know. I was dissatisfied with my life here." He looked toward the trees on the left as if he were searching for something. "What I need cannot be found on Xarta."

What did he need? He didn't want a complete submissive, and he didn't want an unwilling slave. Didn't really leave much choice, did it? She studied his fine ass and sculpted thighs, amazed that a man as beautiful as he would have any sexual interest in her.

He was either a great actor, or he really found her attractive. Irritation swept through her at the realization of being pleased by that.

When she looked over at him again, he had turned, his body even more magnificent in profile. The sharp planes of his chest tapered to a rock-hard abdomen and a cock that any normal, breathing woman would die to call her own.

Yet, despite his aura of power and authority, she sensed a loneliness deep inside him, a need for something, for someone. A need to belong, to be accepted, to share.

A gentle tug squeezed her chest when she looked at him.

No, she was not going to feel anything for Kaden. This was ridiculous. She was no psychic. What did she care what Kaden needed anyway? She had enough trouble figuring out her own happiness, let alone someone else's. Especially someone as complex and foreign to her as Kaden.

"Come here, Marina."

Immediately, she slid off the chaise and moved to him. Kaden opened his hand, revealing the smooth, purple fruit. He tore off a piece.

"Open your mouth."

She did, and he slid the fruit onto her tongue. Drops of the sticky juice dribbled down her chin and onto her chest. She quickly closed her mouth and savored the flavor.

Sweeter than anything she'd ever tasted, it seemed to warm as it slid down her throat. "That's fabulous. What's it called?"

"*Donage*. Prominent in the tropical forests of Xarta, rare in the desert areas. It's quite sought after."

After swallowing, she nodded. "I can understand why."

He pulled another piece and waved it in front of her face. "Open."

She shuddered at the sensual promise in his eyes and opened her mouth. How could the simple act of sliding a piece of fruit between her lips become so erotic? Perhaps because of the way Kaden fed her. Slowly, as if he were easing his cock inside her mouth instead of the sweet purple fruit. More juice fell from his hands onto her chest. She looked down to see lines of purple nectar on her breasts, then held her breath as Kaden bent down and licked a drop from her nipples, then moved his tongue along the trail of purple juice.

Marina shuddered and reached for his head, tangling her fingers into his dark blond hair. She needed his touch, his mouth on her, her body still afire, still on the edge of release. As his tongue roved from one breast to another, she imagined his hot mouth taking her clit and sucking it until she exploded. God, she needed an orgasm!

When Kaden withdrew and stood up, she whimpered in disappointment. One corner of his mouth curled up and he traced her jaw line with his finger. "Not yet, *min so lecheh*. Soon."

"What did you just say?" she asked.

"My sweet fruit."

"Oh." She liked that. "And what does *zejehr* mean?"

"It's an endearment. Sort of like 'my love'."

She absolutely would not think that meant anything other than something he would utter in the heat of passion. No way was she going to let her female mind conjure up a relationship where none existed.

"You have *donage* juice on your chin," he said with a smile.

She raised her hand to wipe it away, but he grabbed her wrist. "No. Let me."

Kaden leaned in and licked the juice from her chin, then moved to the corner of her mouth, his tongue lightly teasing her. He drew back just enough to meet her gaze. His was hot, penetrating, his pupils dilated. His breath, so sweet from the fruit, touched her skin like a soft caress. He bent in and pressed his mouth lightly against hers, rimming her lips with his tongue before sliding it inside her mouth in search of hers.

In a heartbeat she'd lost her breath, lost her senses, lost any hope of acting as if he didn't matter to her. His touch, his taste, everything about him made her want things she'd never wanted before. Was it some sort of magic that Xartanian Doms wielded over their subs? Could she possibly fall in love with a man she barely knew?

No. This was purely physical. She was aching for an orgasm and every time he looked at her, touched her, put his lips anywhere on her body, her nerve endings shrieked for completion. Of course she'd react to his mouth on hers, his arms wrapped around her and crushing her to his hard, naked body. What woman near orgasm wouldn't? She had to quit thinking emotional and start thinking physical.

Starting now. She pushed away so that she could see him. "Kaden, I need an orgasm. Is that going to happen today?"

Arching a brow, he said, "That's for me to decide. Don't bring it up again or you will be punished."

"I thought we were speaking freely right now."

"I have my limits. You want to talk about the case, fine. In any other area, I expect you to respond and act like my sub."

How much more cooperative did she have to be? Murderous intent sailed through her mind, as did the thought of rebelling and just making herself come. Somehow she knew he'd stop that from happening, then make her wait a week while he brought her close time and time again. Could she go insane from a constant state of arousal?

Deciding discretion and cooperation was best at this point, she kept her mouth shut.

Good thing, too, since at that moment two women and one man entered the bathing chamber. All of them were naked, which somewhat lessened her chagrin over being in the same state of undress. Since they didn't seem to be preoccupied with their lack of clothing, she supposed she shouldn't, either.

One woman had long hair the color of a blackbird, her skin like pale cream. The other was completely green from her hair to her skin, though human in appearance. The male was very tall, very broad, with reddish-brown hair that hung almost to his shoulders. He was gorgeous, too, although how anyone could notice anything but his prominently displayed erection she didn't know.

Marina bowed her head in the submissive position, not wanting to call any more attention to herself than necessary. She watched out of the corner of her eye as Kaden approached the male.

"I am Kaden of Xarta."

The other man bowed his head. "I am Jhin of your neighboring planet, Sertal. These are my submissives. The dark-haired woman is Leen, the green-haired woman is Var."

Kaden nodded and pointed to Marina. "This is my newly acquired submissive, Marina. She is of Earth."

Her peripheral vision allowed her to see Jhin assessing her. "She is lovely," he said to Kaden.

"Thank you. Still learning, but she is a quick study."

Marina rolled her eyes at the mirth in his voice. Like she was a dog being trained. Some day she'd make that man pay for being so arrogantly condescending.

"Tell me, Kaden," Jhin said. "Shall we let our women play together? I'm in need of a bit of amusement this morning."

Oh holy hell. What did that mean? If she was going to be ordered to service Jhin, she and Kaden would have words. There were limits to what she was willing to do. She sent mental pleas to Kaden. *Please say no, please say no, please say no.*

Kaden turned his head and glanced at her over his shoulder. *Read my body language, dammit! No, no, no!*

"I think that sounds like a fabulous idea."

Shit.

Chapter Seven

Kaden watched for Marina's reaction. Irritated, definitely. Curious? Possibly. She was too sexually aroused to deny that pleasure of any kind might generate the orgasm she sought.

But she wouldn't climax with anyone but him. Not now, not...

No, he couldn't say "ever". She wasn't with him because she wanted to be, or even because she truly belonged to him.

"Wonderful," Jhin said, his dark eyes gleaming with lust as he looked at Marina.

"A few rules before we begin," Kaden said, motioning Jhin to the far corner of the room. "I have not fucked Marina yet. I'll be the first to do so, so my only request is that you do not touch her." He knew the protocol. Jhin would have to comply. No Dom could take another's sub without the Dom's permission.

Jhin pursed his lips. "I suppose I must honor your request, although I would like to feel her mouth around my cock."

"Some other time, perhaps," Kaden said, finding it difficult to be polite when Jhin was practically drooling.

Jhin turned away and spoke to his women, who stood and nodded, their heads bowed in a position of respect. Kaden moved toward Marina and took her hand, leading her to the edge of the bathing pool. "You need a bath."

She nodded, her head bowed.

"I want to watch Leen and Var bathe you."

Her head whipped up and her eyes widened. She mouthed the word "no".

Kaden frowned. "Marina, assume the position of obedience or I will punish you in front of Jhin and the women."

Her chest rose with her sharp intake of breath. Her mouth set in a grim line. Fury sparking her green eyes into hard points, she dropped her head.

"Shall we bathe?" Jhin asked.

Kaden nodded, leading Marina into the steaming pool. Leen and Var submerged completely, quickly surfacing and pushing their wet hair away from their faces. Jhin whispered to them and inclined his head toward Kaden. They walked through the water and stopped in front of them, their heads bowed.

"What is your pleasure, Sire?" Var asked, her green skin sparkling almost like the emeralds at Marina's breasts.

"Bathe Marina."

"As you wish," Leen said with a quick nod.

The women took Marina's hands and led her to the center of the pool. Kaden settled into a sitting position near the edge of the water, watching as they turned her around to face him, then instructed her to submerge. His breath caught when she sprang out of the water, tossing her dark curls behind her.

Such a contrast the three women were. Marina's bronzed skin, Leen's pale flesh and the green of Var were like a kaleidoscope of color. Even their bodies were different. Where Marina was lush and curvy, Leen was very tall and reed-thin with tiny breasts. Var was small everywhere.

"Look at me, Marina," Kaden commanded, wanting to see her eyes, to gauge if she could let go enough to enjoy the touch of another woman. He suspected she could take pleasure in many sensual delights if she'd only allow herself. And what she enjoyed, he would enjoy also. This lesson was merely a warm-up. Soon, they'd be busy doing other things.

Alone.

But now, he would relish the thought of Marina being pleasured by the two beautiful women bathing her. And hope that he could keep from storming across the bathing pool and fucking her right then. Already his cock was hard, his balls aching as they filled with the come he would soon spill inside her. Perhaps he'd stroke it as he watched the women bathe Marina. Considering she'd be focusing on him, that might add to her enjoyment of what was about to happen.

Marina couldn't believe what Kaden was doing to her. How dare he assume that she'd enjoy frolicking in the water with two other women? He hadn't even asked, just assumed.

Well, of course he assumed. This was all about his pleasure, not hers. He and Jhin would be the ones who got off on this girl-on-girl display. Wasn't that like most men? Their fantasy, to watch women get it on? Well she'd do the bath thing, but she wasn't taking part in anything else.

The pale woman, Leen, smiled at her and reached for a handful of some clear liquid that flowed from the rocks into the pool. Strange that it didn't create any bubbles or discolor the water in any way. Marina inhaled the liquid, sparks of arousal shooting to her sex. Wow, that was some heady soap. The scent was tropical. Gardenias, or maybe some kind of jasmine, with a little musk added in. Some type of aphrodisiac, maybe? Her nipples stood hard, the emeralds vibrating gently.

"Relax, Marina," Leen said, meeting her gaze as she spread the liquid over her shoulders.

"You're allowed to look at me?"

"Why yes," she said, mirth evident in her voice. "All submissives are equal in our sires' eyes. We can speak as long as we are not under an order of silence."

Funny how Kaden hadn't mentioned *that* to her. "I see. I'm new here and don't know the rules yet."

"You will learn soon enough. There is much pleasure to be had here on Xarta," Var added.

Pleasure for the men, Marina thought. But Leen and Var's hands were soft as they massaged the lotion into her arms and shoulders, relaxing away the stress-induced kinks. They seemed to know exactly how much pressure to apply and where. Soon, she was completely comfortable as they worked her upper back with the bathing lotion.

Var moved in front of her and Leen stayed behind, brushing her hair away and working on her shoulders. Var applied more bath lotion and spread the slick liquid over her breasts. Marina's nipples hardened as Var applied soft strokes back and forth, reminding her that she hadn't yet come despite the constant barrage of sensual pleasures Kaden had made her suffer.

And sensual pleasure was what she felt right now. A fact that shocked her. These were women touching her, yet she was not aroused by women. Was it because she hadn't come, that she was in full arousal? She looked at Kaden, his eyes darkening, his hand gently massaging his cock and balls.

He was aroused watching the women bathe her. Did he know how it would make her feel?

She hated to admit that his pleasure in watching them inched her desire up more than a few notches. But it was fact.

Kaden kept his gaze on her as he relaxed upon the ledge of the bathing pool. Jhin reclined across the pool from him. Both men leaned back on their elbows, both spouting impressive erections. But Kaden's was the only cock she focused on, remembering the texture of it as her lips covered it, the taste of it as he came torrents in her mouth. The same cock she had dreamed about while she slept, imagined it thrusting hard inside her juice-filled cunt as she screamed into the night. But she hadn't come then. When would she be able to release this torturous arousal? Hadn't she been punished long enough?

Determined to torment Kaden as much as he'd tortured her, she closed her eyes as Var moved her hands down her ribcage and stomach, the muscles of her abdomen jumping at the woman's touch. Leen moved in and wrapped her arms around Marina, cupping her breasts in her hands. Leen's small breasts slid against Marina's back, her nipples pointed, obviously aroused. Marina looked down and watched Leen circle her nipples with her thumbs, then tug them between her fingers.

Her legs trembled and she focused once again on Kaden. He took his cock into his hand and began to leisurely stroke it from base to tip. The women had guided her to the shallow end of the bathing pool now, so that only her knees and below remained in the water. Var spread Marina's legs apart, and dropped to her knees, using the sweet-scented lotion on her thighs. When she slid her palm between her legs and cupped her aroused sex, Marina whimpered, then captured her bottom lip between her teeth to keep from crying out. Leen continued to massage her breasts and caress her nipples. The sensation of having both these women touch her with their soft, gentle hands was more erotic than she had ever thought possible.

She wished there was a mirror in the room so she could watch the play, wondering how much of a contrast they made with their varying body types and colors. Marina had long ago given up being ashamed of her body. She was simply who and what she was and she would make no apologies for it.

"Lick Marina's pussy," Jhin commanded to Var. He, too, had taken up stroking his shaft with his own hands, the head swelling and growing a dark purple as he clenched it tight.

Var rinsed Marina's sex, then leaned in, her green tongue snaking out to lick at the drops of water along Marina's slit. She cried out at the burning heat of Var's mouth and would have sank to her knees if it weren't for Leen holding onto her.

The alien woman had an incredibly talented tongue, one that any woman would love to have pleasuring them. Marina looked to Kaden, desperate for the orgasm that approached. Kaden removed his hand from his swollen cock and shook his head as he approached them.

"No Marina. You may not come." He motioned the two women aside. They quickly bowed and scurried over to Jhin, who wasted no time in commanding them to suck his cock and balls.

Kaden stepped behind her and turned her toward Jhin and the women. "Watch as they pleasure him," he commanded in a soft whisper. His light beard brushed her neck, sending prickly sensations down her spine and between her legs. He wrapped his arms around her, not touching the places on fire for his hands. His cock nestled at the rise in her buttocks. She desperately wanted to bend over and beg him to fuck her. Fuck her anywhere, and in any way. She just needed to come.

"Not yet," he said as if he sensed her need. "Very soon, Marina. Be patient and watch."

She didn't want to watch. God help her, every cell in her body was screaming at him to fuck her. One or two strokes would be all it took to send her over the edge. Or he could touch her. Hell, at this point she'd probably come if he brushed her nipples with his strong, calloused hands. But watch? No, she wasn't interested in watching someone else get off. Not when she was so close herself. So close, and denied over and over again. She whimpered her frustration when Kaden reached for her right hip, pulling her against the hard length of him.

"You want to come, don't you?" His breathing was harsh and rapid. When she nodded, he said, "Yes, Marina. I do too. I'm dying to shoot my hot come inside that wet pussy of yours. You are wet for me, aren't you?"

"Yes, Sire."

"Is your cunt tight and burning with need for my hard cock, Marina?"

Why was he torturing her like this? Between his words and the way Var completely swallowed Jhin's ten inch cock while Leen licked and suckled his balls, she was nearly mad with passion. The way Kaden touched her but didn't touch her in the right places only made it worse. She sucked in a ragged breath and shuddered as Jhin lifted Var and turned her around, bending her over the ledge of the pool. With one quick thrust he buried his huge shaft between the woman's wide pussy lips. Her roar of pleasure reverberated off the walls of the room. Leen moved to the ledge and situated herself in front of Var, who drove her tongue into the pale woman's pussy like she was starving for its nectar.

Marina couldn't take much more of this, but she knew begging Kaden would get her nowhere. He had to have a will of steel not to fuck her while watching the erotic play in front of them. Then again, *he* had come last night. Twice. She hadn't come in…well, since the last time Kaden had licked to her a mind-numbing orgasm at the restaurant.

What she wouldn't give to have that now. Just one swipe of his tongue against her throbbing clit. One sweep of his hand along her inflamed sex. Anything.

Leen had shifted to a reclining position on the pool deck, her knees bent, her hips rising and falling as she fed Var her sex. Juices poured off Var's chin as she licked at Leen's pussy, her tongue moving up and down so quickly it became a green blur. Sweat poured off Jhin's back as he reared back and thrust forward hard, nearly knocking Var to her knees. But she held onto Leen's thighs and steadied herself. Leen let out a keening wail and flooded Var's face with her come. At that moment, Jhin shuddered and pulled out of Var's pussy. The woman quickly turned around and engulfed his shaft in her mouth as he moaned in orgasm.

The sights, the sounds, the cacophony of ecstatic cries was all too much. Marina's entire body trembled with the need for orgasm. She thought she might just faint if it didn't happen for her soon.

"Now, Marina, it's our turn." Before she could turn around, she was swept into Kaden's arms and carried out of the pool. Using quick strides, he moved down the hallway and entered their rooms, the wall sliding shut behind them.

"Get on your knees and suck me," he commanded, standing in front of the bed with his legs parted and his hands on her hips.

She complied, desperate for a taste of his tangy flavor. Her lips covered the purple head, sealing it off and licking his sweet flavor from the opening. He cursed in his native language and reached for the wet tendrils of her hair, winding them around his hands and pulling her face toward his swollen cock.

"Deeper, Marina. Suck me deeper."

She gave him all that he asked for, and more. Her mind was awash in sensations she couldn't begin to describe. A hunger for Kaden possessed her, causing her limbs to tremble. She'd never wanted anything more than this moment, with this man.

The emerald stones tingled against her nipples, the one at her clit rocking back and forth like a lover's caress. Such slight movement should have made her come, but strangely, they only served to stretch her further on a rack of blinding, near-orgasmic bliss, that place between pleasure and painful arousal that only fulfillment could cure. Such sweet, sweet torment!

Reaching for the twin sacs under Kaden's shaft, she cupped them, massaged them, urged him with her mouth and her tongue to give up their contents. With a low growl, Kaden tipped his head back and gushed into her waiting mouth. She swallowed several times to take in all that he had given her, loving the hot, sweetly spicy taste of him. Finally, he shuddered and pulled away from her, then lifted her to a standing position and crushed his mouth against hers.

That he would kiss her with his taste still lingering on her tongue was magical, erotic, so amazingly sensual that she could have wept. His hands moved over her body, touching her where she'd desperately needed his touch, sweeping over her nipples to flick the charms vibrating the crests into a constant state of exquisite sensation. He moved his other hand between her legs, parting her swollen folds and sliding one, then two, then three fingers into her starving cunt. The muscles of her pussy latched onto his fingers and milked them as if they were his cock.

Right now, they were her salvation, as the first spasms neared.

"Not yet, Marina. Hold back for me," he commanded.

Now she did weep, shook her head from side to side, communicating without words that it would be impossible for her to hold back.

He asked too much of her.

Kaden grabbed her chin and turned her face to meet his heated gaze. "You can, and you will. You will come only when I say so."

Barely able to see through the pool of tears clouding her vision, she nodded, fighting back the waves as he continued to slowly thrust his fingers in and out of her pussy. He was testing her, she knew it. She wanted to give into the need that made her tremble, but she didn't. An insane desire to please him took control, a need to give him what he'd asked of her. She fought the sweeping sensations, pushing them to the back of her mind, thinking of how incredible her orgasm would be once he had his cock buried deep inside her.

His mouth ravaged hers, his tongue fucking her with a rhythm that she was desperate to experience between her legs. Finally, he removed his fingers, her cunt weeping its juices down her thighs.

"Now, Marina. It's time."

Scorching her with eyes that burned with a hunger that surely mirrored her own, Kaden pushed her onto the bed and raised her legs, pressing her further and further into the soft mattress. He bent to take her lips again in a biting kiss that only made her soar higher with the need for completion.

"Fuck me, Marina," he commanded. "Grab my cock with your pussy and fuck me."

With a cry of grateful delight, she lifted her hips and he plunged into her with one hard thrust.

She cried out at the sweet invasion. Oh God. He was huge, filling her completely deeper than she'd ever been filled before. Her pussy fit tightly around him, the sensation causing spasms of amazing, sparkling sensations like nothing she had ever felt before.

Had she ever been fucked? Not like this. Not after holding back for so long it seemed as if she would die from wanting it. Kaden pressed harder against her, nearly splitting her apart as he forced her legs wide and high, so deep she felt him in her belly.

"Are you ready to come for me, *zejehr*?" he asked, his voice tight with drawn passion.

"Yes, Sire, yes! Please let me come!"

He moved back, then thrust again, changing his tempo from quick and hard to light and easy. "Not yet, Marina. Soon."

The tears flowed freely now, a combination of utter frustration and blissful delight. How was she ever going to survive this magic that he bestowed upon her? How had she missed having something like this occur in her life before this moment? Nothing had prepared her for what she was experiencing now. Nothing compared to the monumental emotions pouring through her. She raked her nails down Kaden's arms, oblivious now to whether he would find her disobedient or not. She wanted what he had to give her, and by God he was either going to give it to her or she would take it on her own.

"Now, Marina," he said, grinding his hips against her clit. "Come on my cock."

He hadn't even finished the sentence before the first wave washed over her. Marina tensed and wailed, a sound so deafening she couldn't believe it spilled from her throat. Her cunt clamped down around Kaden's cock, gripping him so tight he could barely move it within her. The scream died in her throat as her voice went hoarse, but still the contractions soared. Relentless, nonstop pleasure filled her, taking him with her as he roared and shot a hot stream inside her.

Their fluids spilled from her contracting pussy and down the crack of her ass, and still her orgasm continued, past the point where she could take in a fresh breath of air, past the point where blinding light obliterated her ability to see, past the point where anything he said made any sense to her. She was dying, literally dying from the pleasure of a nonstop orgasm, one that she had waited an eternity to have, and wasn't going to let it stop until it completely drained her.

Tiny spasms continued as Kaden leaned back and pulled her legs from his shoulders, then collapsed onto the bed, rolling her over to the side. He remained inside her, still stroking small climaxes from her core as he gently pulsed within her.

She continued to come long after she had lost the ability to remain conscious. The last thing she felt was Kaden's cock hardening once again inside her.

Chapter Eight

Kaden let Marina rest for a couple hours before waking her to dress for the main meal in the palace dining room.

She stretched, strangely contented by the soreness in her legs, especially the tenderness between them. She still shuddered at the remembered orgasm, the way Kaden had captured her gaze and held it as he thrust repeatedly inside her with a passion that matched hers.

Now she watched him. His back was turned and she admired the play of muscles as he lifted his shirt over his head to put it on. When he turned to her, she dropped her gaze, whether from obedience or embarrassment at being caught staring, she couldn't say.

"You look beautiful," he said.

"Thank you, Sire." She stared down at the gossamer gown that revealed much more than it hid. A thin gold fabric more like a dense silken net than a dress, it spread to the floor and outward, but the slit ran along both sides all the way up to her neck, the same as the garment she'd had on the night of the auction. A chain belt rested on her hips, preventing the dress from billowing out and showcasing her assets completely.

Not that any were hidden to start with.

The way he looked at her, though, his gaze traveling over every curve, every shadow, made her feel...beautiful.

Which was something she had never felt in the presence of a man. Beautiful, feminine, like a desirable woman. Surprisingly, she enjoyed the feeling. Years of dressing like a man, always having to act tough, had made her somehow forget that she was, indeed, a woman. A woman who frankly enjoyed having a man dominate her, at least in sexual matters. She smiled at the transformation both externally and internally. Who'd have thought she could ever embrace this kind of lifestyle?

"Are you hungry?"

Yes, she was. Hungry for Kaden, starving for what he gave her, as if she'd never get enough of him, no matter how much he fed her. But her stomach rumbled in response. Kaden laughed.

"Good, let's go."

She stepped forward and stopped in front of him, wondering why he was waiting, but knowing she wasn't supposed to ask.

"Look at me," he commanded.

She did, his warm gaze never failing to fire her blood hot and boiling in an instant. Would she ever grow tired of being near him? What would happen when this mission ended and she didn't have him around any longer? In such a short period of time he'd become her entire life.

Stupid. Her bond with him came from being on a planet where she didn't know anyone else, where strange customs abounded and she was no more than a slave. Kaden was her familiarity, her lifeline amidst the unfamiliar, and nothing more.

"I want you to wear this." He removed the plain black collar where he'd attached the leash, replacing it with one of a finely sculpted black leather with emeralds embedded in the front and a ring at the center.

He hooked the leash onto the collar. She wanted to hate the fact that she was controlled, possessed by him. But as he wound the leash around his hand, drawing ever closer to her as he did so, it suddenly became an erotic moment, not an enslaving one.

When he pressed his lips softly against hers, brushing them back and forth lightly, breathing his sweet breath into her mouth, she sighed, more contented than she should be considering the circumstances.

"Shall we eat now?" he asked, his voice low and husky like a jungle cat's purr.

"Yes, Sire," she managed, desperate for some cool liquid to moisten her suddenly dry throat.

Kaden led her down the hallway. She remained a leash-length behind him as he leisurely strolled through the huge palace. She took the opportunity to admire his backside clad in tight black leather, his white sleeveless shirt billowing in the light breeze. A realization hit as she followed him through the palace, knowing that men and women watched them pass.

Not only was he showing her off as his, she was also claiming him as hers. He held the leash and he led her, but she possessed him, owned him, as much as he owned her.

She tipped her head down and allowed a smile of pure feminine satisfaction.

They crossed an open courtyard and entered the tall double doors that led toward the dining hall. Long rows of wooden tables lined the massive room. Already, a multitude of people were present, all dressed similarly to her and Kaden.

They sat at the center table, insinuating themselves between a crowd of people. Marina glanced up at the other women around her, all beauties of varying species and shapes. She no longer felt out of sorts on this planet because she wasn't petite and thin, since there was no ideal type of female body. Instead, it seemed that Xarta celebrated everyone, no matter their appearance.

Kaden nodded to those around him. Marina smiled at the women nearby, including one willowy blonde who was breathtakingly beautiful. The blonde smiled sweetly, then trained her gaze on the plate in front of her. Marina did the same, and while the men conversed, the women ate silently.

"Marina, look up, please," Kaden said.

She did, making eye contact with him.

"I want you to watch the Doms and their subs. Observe and learn from them."

She nodded and looked around, once again making eye contact with the lithe blonde. There was something familiar about her and her dark-haired sire, but she couldn't possibly have met them before. Surveying the room, she watched the way the women acted, their heads bowed, making occasional eye contact only when they were told to by their sires.

A ruckus a few rows down from them caught her attention. She watched in horror as a tall man with a bald, tattooed head yanked a petite woman from the eating bench and dragged her out of the hall. Tears streaked the woman's face as she mumbled almost incoherently about something not being her fault and begged not to be punished.

Marina's heart clenched at the sight of the poor woman being beaten around the buttocks by her Dom. When she fell and he kicked her side, grabbing her to drag her to a standing position, two of the guards she had seen the night of the auction stepped between the sobbing woman and the very angry Dom. One of the guards picked up the woman and led her away, while the other guard exchanged very heated words with the Dom.

"He will lose his sub because of that," Kaden said.

Marina turned to him and frowned, but didn't speak.

"You have a question. Go ahead and ask," he said.

"Why is she being taken from her sire?" Although she was more than relieved to see the woman separated from the man who was clearly abusing her.

"There is a fine line between dominance and getting off on physical abuse. That sire wasn't offering sensual punishment, he was beating his slave. His money will be refunded and he won't be allowed to purchase another female on Xarta."

Good. Marina was sickened by the way he treated his woman. Kaden's comments brought up more questions, but she knew now was not the time to ask. She wanted to ask him about sensual punishment, about the difference between enslaving a woman and mastering her sexually. Was there even a difference? The customs here confused her.

"The reason we remain at the palace after purchasing is so that those who monitor the well-being of submissives can watch the behavior of Doms with their new slaves. Harsh physical punishment beyond what is pleasurable or tolerable is forbidden."

She had so much to learn, starting now as she watched the way the other Doms treated their subs. Some were very tender, stroking their hair and their bodies in incredibly suggestive ways that fired her to a scorching level. She no sooner began to concentrate on the familiar-looking blonde and her sire than Kaden ran his palm over her back.

The possessive sensation of his hand along her spine gave her shivers of delight. His caress was soft, his fingertips lightly feeling their way down her back until he reached her buttocks. When he slid his hand underneath her and cupped her sex, she moistened instantly, the wetness seeping from her pussy.

Kaden used his other hand to stroke her cheek, her jaw line, trailing a fingertip down her throat and between her breasts. The emeralds began to vibrate and her nipples hardened with a painful pleasure.

As he touched her, the dark-haired man and the blonde watched with intent interest. The blonde smiled, and Marina was once again filled with that sense of recognition, as if she should know who the woman was, but she couldn't place her other than as a fragment.

"Your new slave is beautiful," the dark-haired man said to Kaden.

Kaden swept his hand possessively over Marina's hair. "Yes, she is."

"I would like to fuck her."

Marina held her breath waiting for Kaden's response. He answered with a slight smile. "Yes, she's an exceptionally good fuck. But I'm afraid I'm feeling quite possessive right now since she's my new plaything.

Perhaps in a week or so, after I've fucked her for awhile, I'll feel like sharing her."

Did Kaden really feel possessive over her, or was this just an act to protect her from being fucked by another man? He sure hadn't had a problem letting other women touch her.

The dark-haired man licked his lips. "Understandable. She is quite the treasure. I am Telor. This is my submissive, Rora."

Again, that sense of familiarity washed over her, but she shook it off. Obviously the couple must remind her of people she knew.

"I am Kaden and this is Marina."

"Perhaps you would like to watch us engage in sex later." Telor tipped Rora's chin so that she looked up. "My sweet slave here enjoys being watched, and I do so like to indulge her when she's been good."

Despite her wariness, Marina felt her body's response to Telor's suggestion. The thought of watching the handsome man with the raven hair fuck the beautiful blonde was intriguing.

Kaden looked to Marina, then grinned. "I'd say we could all enjoy something like that. I have yet to fuck my woman publicly, and have an urge to do so."

Marina shivered under Kaden's heated gaze. Would he fuck her in public? Her cunt quivered at the thought of having sex with Kaden while another couple watched.

More amazing revelations into her psyche. She was an exhibitionist!

"Tonight, then, in one of the playrooms?" Telor suggested.

Kaden nodded. "I will contact you."

He looked at Marina. "Would you enjoy that, *zejehr*?"

She swallowed and nodded. "Yes, Sire."

"Good." He bent over and licked her neck, sending shivers of ecstasy down her spine. Kaden whispered in her ear. "Keep a look out for the missing women, but try not to give away that you're searching. This is why I've given you permission to look around. Oh, and smile as if I'm whispering something suggestive."

She did, mainly because the feel of his warm breath against her neck was quite suggestive, indeed. Reminding herself she was on a mission and not here just for her pleasure, she straightened and began to search the room.

It was so crowded she couldn't see much of anything other than the people nearby. This wasn't going to work.

"Get up, Marina. I will show you around, introduce you to a few people I know."

She did as Kaden bid, rising and following him as he led her by the leash. He knew that this would be the only way they'd be able to spot the women, if they were even still here at the palace. It had been a month since the last one was taken, so it was possible they were no longer in the palace.

They stopped at a few tables so Kaden could speak to some of the men. While he busied himself talking, Marina took the opportunity to look around the room in search of the missing women.

No luck. How were they ever going to find the women on this planet? She sure hoped Kaden had an idea, because she didn't have a clue.

* * * * *

Kaden led Marina out of the palace, taking the moving walkway that would lead them through the city. He watched her as she took in the pink skies and tall buildings made of material known only to Xarta. Flexible buildings to withstand their seasonal winds, they swayed from side to side in the breeze.

Marina's eyes widened and she looked as if she wanted to say something.

"You have my permission to speak, Marina. We're alone now, so you don't have to ask."

"The buildings move."

"Yes."

"Can those inside feel the movement?"

"No. We have stabilizers built into the structures so that what you see is not felt. We have very strong windstorms here a few months every year."

"Fascinating."

He pointed out the various trees and shrubbery, so different in size, color and texture than the native plants on Earth. Where on Earth things were green, on Xarta pastels colored the landscape around her. Marina was fascinated, asking question after question.

"Did you spot any of the women while we were in the dining hall?"

She shook her head. "No. If they're not in the palace, how will we find them?"

"I have a few people looking. They know what questions to ask. It's possible they will show at the gathering."

"What's a gathering?"

"A grand party at the palace to celebrate the coming season. In fact, it's a prime opportunity to enact the second part of our plan."

"You mean try to find the method of transport of the slaves?"

"Yes. They always bring new slaves in during the gathering. We just have to figure out how they're getting here, and who's bringing them in. It's a part of the puzzle we haven't yet been able to discover."

"I wish I could remember, Kaden, but I only get vague images when I try to recall what happened to me."

"We can work on that. I figured the women who were taken had been drugged, and obviously with a chemical compound used here in Xarta that affects short-term memory."

"Any way to get those memories back?"

"The only way to do that is to keep pushing your mind to remember that night you were taken."

"I went to the BDSM club. That much I remember."

"Did you meet anyone?"

She shook her head. "I don't know. I remember dancing, but I can't place with whom. Everything after that is a blank until I woke up here. Although…"

"What?"

"When I woke here, I didn't have the equilibrium dizziness I get from space travel."

"Spaceship travel, you mean?"

"Yes. Other than feeling a little groggy, I was fine."

"So you didn't come by ship."

She shrugged. "I don't know. I might have, and maybe I didn't experience the dizziness because I was unconscious."

Kaden smiled and nodded as another couple passed by. As soon as they were out of earshot, he said, "Could be a portal."

"I hadn't thought of that. An opening between Earth and Xarta?"

"Yes. We need to figure out if there is one, and if there is, I'd bet it's near the intake quarters for new slaves. The key is to find the doorway."

"Okay. How do we do that? If there's a portal, they're not just going to let us step up to it and walk through."

"No, but if we gain their trust, try to involve ourselves in their 'recruiting' of slaves, we'll be able to see it."

"How do you intend to manage that?"

Kaden grinned. "Easy. I'll offer myself up as a recruiter. I'll tell them you're happy with your new surroundings, and you know of several Earth women they could bring over."

Marina smiled, her entire face lighting up. "Great idea. Risky, though."

"True enough."

"I wish I could get this block out of my memory. If I knew who took me, it would at least be a start in unraveling the chain."

"Keep trying. It'll come back to you." Kaden pulled a berry from a nearby bush and popped it into his mouth.

"What's that?"

He grabbed a handful from a nearby *blue* bush. "Fruit. Everything is ready for harvest now."

Marina's eyes widened when he placed the bursting green berry into her mouth. "Oh my God, what is this?"

"*Lnxtar*. Another one of our sweet fruits. This is what our gathering celebrates. When all the fruits are ripe on the trees, the crops that take a year to grow are ready for harvest." At her frown, he grinned. "We do other things on Xarta besides just fuck, Marina. Xarta is an agricultural planet. Our soils are rich and our crops are heralded through the galaxies."

"I had no idea. That purple fruit from the trees was very good, too."

He laughed. "Yes, it looked good dribbling down your chin and over your breasts, too. I enjoyed licking the juices from your nipples."

Those very nipples beaded under her gossamer dress, clearly delineating the puckered areolas. He sent vibrations to the nipple charms, and a stronger one to her clit. Marina gasped. "Don't do that."

Without the forced submission, she was quite feisty. He had to admit he kind of liked her this way. Then again, he liked her under his control, too. "I do what I please, Marina. You know that."

"It makes me horny, dammit."

Her frustration and arousal pleased him. What a remarkable woman she was. He would miss her greatly when their mission was over. Maybe more than he should. "I'm preparing you for what is to come later."

She glanced up at him. "And what is that?"

"Our time with Telor and Rora."

She swallowed, hard, and blinked. "You like watching other people have sex, don't you?"

"Yes. Voyeurism is quite stimulating." He stopped and turned her to face him. "You like it too."

"I don't know," she said, turning her gaze away from him. Her musky scent filled the air around them. She was aroused.

"Yes, you do know. I don't understand why you deny your sexual urges, Marina. You're a very sensual woman. I think you enjoy voyeurism, and if I guess correctly, a bit of exhibitionism, too."

She shrugged. "I'm just doing my job."

"Don't deny to me how you feel."

Lifting her chin, she said, "This is just another undercover assignment, Kaden. Don't read too much into my actions."

Something bothered her. Why was she trying to hide the fact that she found her situation arousing? "There's no shame in being a submissive, Marina."

"I'm submissive to no one, Kaden. This is an act, remember?"

"It wasn't an act when you came all over my cock," he said, feeling the stirrings of desire for her. She made him insane with lust to the point he wanted to do nothing but fuck her all the time.

She shrugged but didn't say anything in response.

"Look at me," he commanded.

She did, the fire in her eyes telling him that she fought her own feelings.

"Admit that you're enjoying this role you play."

"No."

"Marina, didn't I tell you that I didn't want to hear that word from you?"

"We're not under watch right now, Kaden. I don't have to play the submissive with you."

"Oh, but you do. As long as we're on this planet, you're mine. I command you, I tell you what to do, and you will do it."

"Fuck off, Kaden. I'm in no mood for this today."

Was she deliberately baiting him, hoping for a reaction? If so, she'd succeeded. He wound the leash around his fist and pulled her to him. "Are you begging for punishment today, Marina?"

She didn't answer, but her eyes spoke volumes.

Desire, need, and an internal war that she was losing.

When would she realize that when she accepted what she was, she would be the winner?

"Answer me."

Again, she said nothing.

"You know what happens when you disobey me."

"I tire of playing this stupid game with you, Kaden."

Emotions swirled within him. Anger that she refused to accept what she was mixed with a heady ache in his groin that only Marina could assuage.

"I warned you not to disobey me. Now you will be punished." He turned on his heel and strode quickly back to the palace. Tethered to the leash, Marina had no choice but to follow. He felt the daggers of her gaze on his back, but he was long past the point of caring.

His mind was already plotting her punishment, one that he, and she, would derive great pleasure from.

Chapter Nine

Marina struggled as Kaden led her back into the palace, his strides quick and purposeful. She had to nearly run to keep up with him.

She didn't want this. Didn't want this game anymore, or the feelings that Kaden forced her to face.

This was a job. Only a job. For him, as well as for her. Oh sure, they'd had great sex, but she was not a submissive. Never had been, never would be.

Frustration filled her. She wanted her freedom, wanted to go back to her solitary, orderly, boring life back on Earth and get as far away as possible from the heady sensations she'd been forced to endure on Xarta.

The realization that this farce could go on longer than she'd anticipated finally hit her when she couldn't spot any of the women at the dining hall. Coupled with the walk she'd taken with Kaden, the delightful smells and sights of Xarta, and she found herself suddenly feeling…comfortable in her position and surroundings.

Strange emotions had filled her then, her heart swelling with an indefinable sensation, then quickly replaced with a cold fear that had left her shaken.

Marina had never been in love. She was over thirty years old and she'd never loved a man. Yet being with Kaden felt right. His tenderness, his passion…yes, even the way he dominated her…did strange things to her mind.

She was beginning to like all this, and that scared the shit out of her. She was starting to have strong emotional feelings for Kaden that went beyond simple lust, and that frightened her even more. How stupid to fall in love with the one man she could never have a future with.

Although how she could love a man who was currently pulling her through the palace hallways was mystifying. He strode quickly past their room and continued down the long hallway, nearly dragging her in his wake. He stopped at a huge doorway, pressing his fingers inside the pad. The door slid open and he pulled Marina inside.

Holy shit! What the hell was all this stuff?

They'd entered a room filled with bondage devices. Shackles on the walls, tables with restraints, a rack filled with different types of whips, gags and a few other things Marina didn't want to even guess about.

Heat settled low in her belly and her sex hummed to life with steady vibrations of excitement. She realized that her mouth was open and she was panting lightly.

What the hell had happened to her in this place? The thought of being restrained, of having Kaden punish her, turned her on more than she ever thought possible. This wasn't who she was. She was a vanilla sex and simple vibrator girl, not some kinky sex goddess who got off on being bound and spanked.

Wasn't she?

She really didn't know anymore.

You're stronger than this, Marina. You can fight it. You don't want this, or the things Kaden makes you feel.

"You need to learn the ways of our people, Marina. A submissive never argues with her Dom."

No way would she respond. She was already in enough trouble, but dammit she couldn't handle the way he made her feel.

He pulled her over to a well-cushioned table about waist-high and two feet wide. It stood in the middle of the room and had restraining cuffs on each end plus on the floor.

"This is what you will face each time you disobey me," he said, his voice bearing no sympathy. "Now, undress, and do it quickly."

She thought of defying him, but what was the point? Her body was already aflame with need for whatever punishment he'd thought up. She'd simply close off her emotions and enjoy the physical aspect of this game with Kaden.

Face it, Marina. You want to be punished. You crave it like an addiction.

How quickly her life, her very way of thinking, had changed. It scared the hell out of her, yet made her want to do whatever he asked of her.

With quick movements, she untied the belt around her waist and pulled the garment free of her body, leaving her naked under his raking gaze. Her traitorous nipples responded by puckering, tightening as the emeralds tingled against her skin.

He purposely made the emeralds vibrate, knowing how it aroused her. The stone at her clit rubbed the tiny nub, sparking it to life. Moisture beaded between her legs.

She should be afraid, considering some of the devices in this room, their express purpose to cause pain of differing levels. Yet the only thing she felt was excitement.

Because she trusted Kaden. He would never hurt her. Nothing he'd done to her so far had been painful. Torturous, yes, but a sweet, aching torment that left her wanting more.

He positioned her over the table, locking the padded restraints around her wrists and ankles. She could only imagine how she looked in this position—bent over, spread-eagled and exposed in every way imaginable.

"Comfortable?" he asked.

"Yes." She grit her teeth, not knowing what to expect.

"Sire."

"Yes, Sire." Sometimes she hated him a lot more than she desired him.

"Do you understand what punishment means in the context of a dominant and submissive relationship?"

"Not really, Sire."

He stepped in front of her, lifting her chin to meet his stern look. "You're about to find out."

But instead of moving behind her to spank her or whatever he was about to do, he stayed in front of her, and slowly began to undress. Her mouth went dry as he lifted the shirt over his head, revealing his perfectly formed torso. She dug her nails into her palms, desperately wishing she were untethered so she could run her fingers over his broad shoulders and muscled chest.

Her gaze traveled to the line of golden hair leading into his pants. He snapped open the pants and slid them down his chiseled thighs. His already stiff cock stood inches away from her mouth.

"Would you like a taste, Marina?"

"Yes, Sire."

Taking his shaft in hand, he stroked it slowly, then moved toward her, drawing close enough for her to lick at the drop of pre-come that appeared. She shuddered at the brief taste he allowed before pulling away and moving behind her.

Something about hearing him back there, but not knowing what he was doing, was quite disconcerting.

"Punishing a submissive is all about emotion, Marina. The only pain involved is the pleasurable kind, and no more than what you can safely tolerate. Do you trust me?"

She inhaled sharply at the feel of his hand caressing her buttocks. "Yes, Sire."

"Good." She knew he smiled, even though she couldn't see his face. "Remember that when this begins. I don't want you to speak unless I ask you to. If you feel more pain than you can handle, you are allowed to say the word 'Xarta' and I will stop immediately."

She nodded, feeling comforted by having a safe word, although she knew he wouldn't deliberately hurt her.

Anticipation filled her. What would he do, how would this play out? Would he use his hand as he was doing now, or something else?

Her question was answered when he walked to a rack in front of her and stood there perusing the punishment objects. Canes, whips, quirts, floggers, even leather straps were lined up neatly in rows.

"Close your eyes, Marina," Kaden commanded, his back still to her.

She didn't want to. She wanted to see what he chose, so she'd know what would happen. But she did as he asked, squeezing her eyes shut.

A minute later, his voice resounded behind her. "Now you can open your eyes. Do you know what I'm going to do to you?"

She nodded.

"I'm going to punish you for disobedience. You need to learn what is and isn't acceptable to me, Marina."

She flinched at the first touch, then relaxed as she realized it was nothing more than his hand caressing her calves. He squeezed the muscles there gently, almost like a massage. Working his way upward, he worked her thighs next, lingering near her sex as he pressed in and rubbed her skin. She felt the moisture at her slit as his fingers dipped between her legs, lightly brushing against her swollen nether lips.

"Your body was made for me, *zejehr*. Supple, strong, curvaceous, just the way I like a woman. I love the way your thighs squeeze me when I'm inside you, pulling my cock in deeper, holding me in place while I fuck that delectable cunt of yours."

He cupped her buttocks, gently squeezing the globes, his fingers trailing a blazing fire as they dipped between them, sliding ever so slowly toward her aching center. He swept his fingertips along her slit and she shuddered, biting back the moan that threatened to escape her lips. The emerald charm tingled against her clit. God, she was close to orgasm already. How could he do this to her with nothing more than a simple caress, so brief she wasn't certain if it had even happened.

The light touch of his hand against her skin lulled her into complete relaxation. But then she felt something that wasn't his hand.

Soft tendrils moved up her legs and across her buttocks, the tails brushing her sex before continuing up her back. So light she could barely feel it, yet deliciously silken against her aroused skin. Kaden followed the tails of the flogger with his hand, the dual sensation of suede and skin warming her blood, making her skin tingle in anticipation.

The first crack of the flogger along her thighs was light, enough to know she'd been swatted, but not painful. The second one landed on her buttocks, still light and easy. Each time he wielded the flogger, it landed in a different spot, so she couldn't anticipate the sting. Her back, her thighs, her buttocks, one after another in rhythmic motions, first light, then stinging sharp, all serving to heighten her anticipation of the next one. The gentle whipping aroused her more and more with each flicking bite of the flogger.

The sensation was way more pleasurable than she had thought it would be. She had prepared herself for a stinging spanking, but nothing had primed her for the arousing feel of her skin coming alive under Kaden's expert touch.

She began to squirm against her bonds as he stroked harder. Stinging slaps of leather burned against her ass, and she found herself lifting her buttocks as if to draw closer to the source of sweet pain. Her pussy was wet, hot, fierce desire coiling deep in her belly as the emerald charm vibrated rhythmically against her clit.

Kaden moved in front of her, the tails of the brown suede flogger resting in his hands. He tipped her chin so she could look at him, then arched a brow, his lips curled in a feral smile. "You like being punished, don't you?"

She didn't answer. She didn't need to. Surely Kaden could read the desire on her face, the lust in her eyes, the need to have him thrust his cock in her pussy and end the aching need thrumming inside her.

"Suck me, Marina."

Finally, she could touch him in a way that truly pleased her. To show him that she was his to command, to break free of the control she'd held onto for so long and give herself up to his pleasure and his alone. How could she have known that allowing him to dominate her would bring her such pleasure?

Kaden held his breath as Marina opened her mouth and surrounded the head of his cock with her lips. Her tongue rimmed the head, licking at the drops of fluid that had gathered there. Watching the thick head disappear between her luscious lips had his balls tightening. Precome spilled into her heated mouth and he fought to hold back.

Truth was, he could release down her throat right this instant. The sight of her pinkened ass cheeks and the way she arched into the swats was enough to drive him over the edge. Never had he been with a woman so responsive to punishment.

Oh, he hadn't hurt her, and he knew it. He wielded a flogger well, and he knew how to follow a woman's lead. He knew how to gauge what was pleasurable and what was too much. Marina either had a high tolerance for pain, or she really got off on it, because she'd demanded much more than he thought she would. So much, in fact, that tiny welts had popped up on her back, buttocks and thighs. Yet not once had she flinched, cried out or uttered the safe word.

Instead she had moaned, whimpered, mewled and made other noises that had his lust factor kicked into overdrive. How he'd kept from having her suck him or plunging his shaft between her red ass cheeks was more than he could fathom.

He needed her in a way that made no sense. But he'd long ago given up trying to figure out his attraction to Marina. She wasn't the type of woman he went for, she wasn't a natural submissive and she had no intention of remaining in his life once this was over.

And he'd never wanted a woman more.

Brushing the hair away from her face, he grasped her head and directed his cock between her full lips, watching as inch by inch his shaft disappeared inside her mouth. Her low moan vibrated against his shaft, forcing him to clench his jaw and hold back the impending torrential release.

He leaned over her and reached for her buttocks, sliding his fingers between the bronzed globes. Wetting fingers with her flowing nectar, he moved upward against her tight hole. She gasped and whimpered against his cock as he slid one finger inside her ass.

She was tight, hot, pulsing around him as if she were already climaxing. He knew what he wanted. He also knew exactly what she needed.

Removing his cock from her mouth, he moved behind her, admiring the moisture flowing down her legs, the way her cheeks were spread, revealing her nether region to him.

"I want that ass, Marina."

She made no response, but her shudders and panting breaths told him she wanted the same thing.

He set the flogger aside and positioned himself between her spread legs, reaching for her glistening slit, groaning as he felt her heat and moisture. She was swollen, hot and ready for him to penetrate her.

Unable to resist, he probed her pussy with the head of his cock, rubbing against her clit and feeling the vibrations of the emerald stone. He closed his eyes and enjoyed the pleasurable sensation, realizing that this is what she felt when the jewel hummed.

"I'm going to fill you, Marina. Your ass, your pussy, everywhere I can, over and over again."

She had learned her lesson well, because she didn't respond. But her pussy did, squeezing the head of his shaft tight as he slid partly inside. Her heat burned him, made him seek her depth, her flame, and he thrust hard, burying his cock inside her cunt.

Marina cried out and arched her back toward him, telling him without words that she wanted more. He held tight to her hips and thrust again, pulled out again, maintaining a rhythm that had her juices pouring over his balls and thighs. He felt the tightening, the enormous pressure of an impending climax, and withdrew, not wanting to end this too soon. As he left her, she whimpered.

He went to the drawer holding the toys and made his choice, smiling at the thick, lifelike cock that he would soon plunge into her swollen cunt.

He turned to her, smiling at the way her eyes widened when she saw what he held in his hands. "I told you I'd fill you completely, Marina. Are you ready? You may answer me now."

Her emerald eyes glittered with lust-filled anticipation. "Yes. Please, Sire."

Settling himself between her thighs again, he wet his fingers with her nectar and drew it upward over her puckered hole, his cock straining with the need to be buried inside her ass. He could already feel how tight she'd be as he slid one finger inside her and spread her juices within.

First he'd spear her pussy with the thick dildo, which was now warm and throbbing like a real cock. He teased her clit and slit with it first, and she spread her legs wider, pushing her ass against him.

Kaden grinned. His woman was hot and ready to be fucked. He wished there were two of him so he could fill her mouth with his length at the same time he filled her ass. But that was not to be. Instead, he'd satisfy himself by stretching her ass and pussy. Working the dildo inside her slowly, she moaned with every inch of the long, thick object, crying out when he finally thrust it deep. He knew that once inside, it would fill her, form itself to the shape necessary to please her, then pulse against the walls of her pussy and shift back and forth like the slow thrusting of a cock.

The dildo would pleasure her, take her to the edge, then leave her teetering, balancing on the precipice.

Then, Kaden would make her come.

Chapter Ten

The pressure was nearly unbearable, a sweet torment that drove Marina ever higher toward the climax she craved.

The dildo that Kaden slipped in her was hot like a real cock, and the damn thing moved so slowly she wanted to scream at it to fuck her hard and fast.

But that wasn't what she really wanted. What she wanted was Kaden's cock buried in her ass. To be filled and fucked in both places, to come like she had never come before.

Her mind shut down all logical thought and focused only on the sensations. Her skin was on fire, sensitized after the sensuous flogging. Every nerve ending in her body was raw, aroused, and she was desperate for an orgasm.

"I'm going to fuck your ass, Marina. You will not come until I tell you."

Damn him! She could have cried at the frustration of being forced to hold back. If this was anything like the last time, she might not survive it.

He swiped her juices over the puckered entrance and she forced herself to relax. She'd never been fucked in the ass with a real cock before, and she wanted Kaden to be the first.

Hell, she wanted him to be the only. Now, and always.

The thought brought tears to her eyes. Tears that she forced back, concentrating instead on preventing the orgasm that hovered so close she could easily will her way into the throes of ecstasy.

She relaxed as she felt the head of his cock probe her tight entrance, needing him to fill her, welcoming the delicious pain that came when he gently forced past the barrier of her sphincter muscles and slid partially inside her.

It hurt. It burned. She tensed, breathing out and trying to deal with the invasion. Kaden's cock was longer, thicker than anything she'd ever put in there before. She couldn't take it all.

But at the same time, she felt the pleasure, little tingling sparks that sent wondrous sensations to her cunt. She focused on that alone.

Her anus contracted around his invading shaft, and she clenched her fingers against her palms, forcing herself to relax. Excitement and trepidation warred within her. She wanted this so badly, wanted it to be good for him.

Because when it was good for Kaden, it was exceptional for her.

He paused, waiting for her body to adjust to the invasion of his thick cock. Her pussy throbbed as the dildo expanded and moved gently back and forth, and she began to relax.

Kaden pulled back and thrust deeper this time. Her skin broke out into goose bumps at the intensity of the sensation as the dildo suddenly moved in rhythm. When he pushed forward, the dildo pulled back a bit. When Kaden pulled back, the dildo moved forward.

Having his cock buried in her ass was nothing like having a toy there. It pulsed with life, moved with a rhythm that sent her soaring into the galaxies. Splinters of need forced her to move back against him, needing much more of what he was giving her.

Marina whimpered and dug her nails into the cushion, shaking her head back and forth as she tried to hold off her orgasm.

"You're tight, Marina. So tight, so hot, like I knew you would be. You're burning my cock, *zejehr*. I'm on fire."

Kaden's words, spoken in such a dark and husky tone, were her undoing. Now that she'd adjusted to his thick shaft inside her ass, she pushed back against him again, needing him to fuck her harder, wanting to scream at him to stab his thick cock deeper and deeper inside her, to make her howl with the pleasure she knew he'd bring her.

This is what had been missing in her life. Fiery sex with someone who knew her body, who knew what she needed even better than she knew. Kaden read her as if he'd spent a lifetime studying her body and her sexual needs. And with that knowledge she relaxed and gave up all of her control to him.

He must have sensed her acquiescence because he growled and wound his hand in her hair, pulling back sharply. The stinging sensation only aroused her more and she bucked against him, demanding that he give her what she wanted. She couldn't ask for it, but she could damn well show him what she needed.

His balls slapped against her pussy, his body tensing as he dug the fingers of his free hand into her hips.

"Now, Marina!" he shouted. "Come for me now!"

She sobbed in blissful relief and let go, her orgasm a torrential downpour as it washed over her, soaking both of them with her come. Kaden groaned and shot hot liquid in her, pumping rapidly back and forth, then collapsing on top of her and winding his fingers through hers as they rode out the intense sensations together.

Her come flooded over the dildo. She felt the object becoming smaller, loosening, and still the contractions held tightly to it and to Kaden's cock.

He panted heavily against her, rubbing her hands with his palms. His body was rigid and tense as he continued to pump his seed deep inside her. He pressed himself firmly against her, his sweat-soaked chest covering her back. Finally, he began to relax, as did she, the tremors milder now, but still racking her body with tiny pulses. She shuddered, the tears continuing to flow down her cheeks.

Her body had gone limp. She barely noticed Kaden pulling out of her, removing the dildo and unfastening the bonds. He drew her upright, massaging the center of her back, relieving the cramping sensation of having been bent over for so long.

She had no complaints. She'd gotten exactly what she'd deserved, and more than what she could have ever hoped for. Kaden turned her to face him and swept her hair away from her face, using his thumb to wipe the last traces of tears from her cheeks. He leaned in and brushed his mouth against hers, so tenderly the tears pooled anew.

Then he swept her into his arms and carried her into the bathing chamber, stepping into the heated water while still embracing her. He sat on the edge of the tub and cradled her head against his chest, using his hands to draw water and pour it over her shoulders and breasts. All the while he remained as silent as she, lightly kissing her head and smoothing her hair with his hand.

If this was punishment, if this was what it was like to be a man's submissive, then she wanted this lifestyle.

No, that wasn't right. She wanted this, but she wanted it with Kaden and no one else.

"Are you all right?" he whispered, pressing his lips against her temple.

"Yes, Sire."

"I can't get enough of you, Marina. I want you again."

She tilted her head to meet his gaze. Hot, desire etched in the creases along his eyes and half-smile. She felt his heat, shocked when her own arousal began anew.

Shifting her in his lap, he turned her so her back rested against his chest. Then he spread her legs and draped them over each of his thighs, exposing her pussy. A building tension coiled deep in her belly, the emerald stone rocking rhythmically against her clit.

Kaden moved his hands over her shoulders, then her breasts, cradling the globes within his palms. In this position she could look down and watch his thumbs flick over her nipples, the sensation arcing straight to her cunt. Instinctively she lifted her hips, craving his touch where she ached the most.

He toyed with her, moving from her breasts to her waist, resting his fingers on her hips, then lightly pulling her against his ever-growing erection. He palmed her thighs, sweeping his hands lightly over her skin before dipping between her legs and touching her inner thighs, so close to her pussy that if she turned sideways, he'd find the mark.

Closer, just a few inches closer and he'd be touching her swollen slit. If only he'd—

"There you are," said a deep male voice behind them.

Marina jerked and tried to leap off Kaden's lap as Telor and Rora entered the bathing chamber. But Kaden held her tightly against him. "There's no need for you to move away," he whispered in her ear.

Feeling incredibly exposed, heat burned her cheeks as Telor and Rora disrobed and entered the bath. Telor was thinner than Kaden, and not nearly as muscular, yet had a finely sculpted body and an erect cock that would make any woman's mouth water. Rora was slender, with large breasts and prominent, coral pink nipples. She was truly lovely with her waist-length, straight blonde hair and long legs.

Marina would have thought she'd have been past worrying about her nudity by now, but this was a bit different. Her legs were widespread, her pussy open for their viewing.

Rora smiled at her as she crept closer, bowing her head toward Kaden. "Sire," she whispered.

"Rora, Telor," Kaden said. "Are you here to watch?"

Marina's pulse raced, her nipples puckering as Telor and Rora smiled at her.

"We would very much like to watch," Telor said, reaching for Rora and grasping her nipples between his fingers. Rora moaned, her eyes darkening, her full lips parting as she began to breathe heavily. She wore piercings also, only hers were smaller, with a black bead dangling from either end of the silver bar embedded in the pink crests. As she spread her legs, Marina saw the same type of piercing in Rora's clitoral hood.

Kaden resumed touching her, reaching for her breasts again, finding the piercings and sliding them through her nipples. The vibrations coupled with his movements of the silver circlets had her gasping, her pussy flooding with arousal. He continued to tease the dark crowns with one hand, the other snaking its way over her belly and searching out her clit. The emerald stone thrummed slowly as if in answer to his questing fingers.

A secret thrill soared through her when he parted the folds of her slit and slid one finger inside, knowing that Telor and Rora could clearly see what he was doing. They watched intently as he casually stroked her slit, rimming her clit with his fingertip. Telor squeezed Rora's breasts, plucking at her nipples until the buds stood out.

Marina wasn't sure if she was more turned on by what Kaden did to her, or by watching Telor and Rora.

"Voyeurism is very exciting, isn't it, Marina?"

"Yes…Sire." She'd almost forgotten to address him correctly, but when she did, he rewarded her by sliding two fingers inside her cunt. She held tightly onto his arms, lifting her ass off his legs to impale her pussy onto his fingers.

"Do you want me to fuck you, Marina?"

She looked at Telor and Rora's faces. Rora's glassy-eyed expression reflected her ecstasy as Telor sat her on his lap, positioning her the same way Marina was positioned. Her legs were spread wide, her bare pussy open to Marina and Kaden's view. Telor plunged two fingers between the folds of her swollen slit, pumping quickly. Rora moaned, licking her lips, not once taking her eyes off Kaden and Marina.

"Yes, Sire. I need your cock inside me, please."

Kaden lifted and held her while she positioned herself over his hard shaft. She slid down slowly while he held her buttocks, squeezing the tender flesh as she fit herself over him.

He filled her completely this way, his thick member stretching her vaginal walls. She felt his length touch her womb, sending sparks of intense pleasure shooting through her core.

"Touch yourself while I fuck you, Marina," Kaden commanded. "I want you to make yourself come."

Grateful that he hadn't asked her to hold off her orgasm, she reached between her parted legs and felt for the vibrating charm at her slit. This was the first time since she had been brought here that she'd been allowed to touch her own pussy, and she found she enjoyed having a completely bare mound. Her skin felt silky, and it was easy to slide her fingers over her clit and stroke the swollen folds. She touched Kaden's shaft, rimming it with her fingers and following his movements as he thrust deep, then partially withdrew.

Rora began to mimic her movements, reaching between her own legs and thrumming her clit with fast, side-to-side strokes. Marina felt as if she was looking at a mirror. She watched in rapt fascination as Telor's shaft disappeared between Rora's pussy lips. Did she and Kaden look similar? It was so strange to watch Rora get fucked by Telor, and to know exactly what she was feeling.

Kaden speared her hard and she whimpered, once again moving her fingers toward her clit and circling the swollen nub that appeared from beneath its cloak. She ground her pussy against Kaden's cock, rewarded with his throaty groan. His fingers dug into her hips and he lifted her up and down on his shaft, nearly slamming her down with a painful force that sent tremors coursing through her.

Between his movements, the visual display before her and her own fingers stroking her clit, she felt her orgasm fast approaching. Kaden must have felt it, too, because he quickened his pace, lifting his hips to drive hard and fast into her.

Telor let out a loud cry and tensed at the same time Rora screamed in ecstasy.

Marina held on, waiting for Kaden to give his permission, knowing now that the longer she waited, the better it would be.

"I feel you, *zejehr*, I feel your orgasm nearing," Kaden whispered. "Let go for me and come on my cock."

His words were the magic key to unlock her response. She tightened around him as the first waves crashed over her. Kaden tensed and dug his fingers even deeper into her hips as his hot semen poured into her. She screamed her climax, bucking against him while she continued to strum her clit.

For awhile afterward, the only sounds were four sets of rapid breaths. Marina leaned forward, resting her hands on her knees. She heard the sounds of Telor and Rora exiting the bathing pool, but she was too exhausted to even speak to them.

Kaden withdrew and lifted her into a standing position, turning her around and kissing her tenderly.

"You have had a long day, my slave," he murmured against her lips. "It's time for us to rest."

He led her out of the pool and into their room, where they slid into bed. Kaden wrapped his arms around her and stroked her back while she listened to the rhythmic sound of his breathing.

Her life had changed in so many ways the past few days. What she thought she'd feel during this assignment was nothing like what had actually happened. Kaden had brought her out of her self-imposed shell and had taught her more about her body and her sexuality than she had ever thought possible.

What would she do when this was over and she had to go back to life the way it was before?

What would she do when she didn't have Kaden next to her every hour of the day?

She couldn't, wouldn't think of that right now. By the time the mission came to an end, she'd have things sorted through in her mind. Right now, her thoughts were jumbled and she was more confused than she'd ever been about any aspect of her life.

When the mission was over, she'd worry about what happened next. For now, she'd enjoy the moments they had together.

The mission! Oh God! She tensed as a flood of memories came back.

She remembered! And she had to tell Kaden what she knew. But were they being monitored, even in the dark of night while they slept?

Turning to face him, she nuzzled his neck, wanting to get close enough to his ear to whisper to him.

He groaned when her leg brushed his cock. She felt it stir to life, and smiled in the darkness. Yes, she was his submissive, but she wielded a considerable amount of power, too. The power to arouse him. Heady stuff, indeed.

She surged against him, knowing she couldn't speak unless he gave her permission. And dammit, she *really* needed to talk.

He wound his fingers in her hair. "Is there something you want, *zejehr*?" he asked, husky promise in his voice.

"Yes, Sire, but not right now. I remembered something about my kidnapping."

His hand stilled in its wandering through her hair.

"Can we speak here?"

He turned to face her. "Yes, but you must whisper and not move too much. Monitors will detect excessive movement and they will begin watching and listening. Tell me what you remember."

"Telor and Rora were the couple I met at the BDSM club the night I was kidnapped. Rora offered me a drink, something really sweet, then she and I danced and Telor watched. Then I remembered getting really dizzy. Telor picked up me up and carried me outside, and the next thing I remember was waking up in the slave area at the palace here."

"So Telor and Rora are part of the trade. You did well to remember. They obviously showed interest in you so they could gauge whether or not you would recall anything about your kidnapping."

"It would seem so."

"Good. Do not let on that you recognize them. Tomorrow night is the gathering party for new submissives. I think its time we put our plan into motion."

Finally able to grab onto something not related to her feelings for Kaden, she felt the excitement fill her. Work had always been her salvation, her only love, and she clung to that with near desperation. "We need to find out the location of the portal, if there is one, and who is bringing the slaves in on this end. I would think Zim is part of this, being the slave master. He has to know where these women are coming from."

"True enough," Kaden said. "And it could be that he, Telor and Rora are the only ones involved in the kidnapping of Earth women. Zim wields much power on Xarta. His motives would never be questioned. Xartanian men assume only that the women brought in as slaves are there because they wish to be enslaved, that they want to be forced. They would not know that these women are brought against their will, which is against the laws of our planet."

"Don't the women tell their Doms that they've been kidnapped?"

"That I don't know. Even if they did, it is part of the slave mystique, a role playing if you will. The Doms would only think it was part of the submissive's wish to be taken against their will, so they would not believe the woman's story to be true."

No wonder the slave traders had been so successful. It was a perfect setup.

"Sleep now, *zejehr*. Tomorrow we will take a walk through the city and formulate our plan when we can talk with more ease."

He kissed the top of her head and gathered her against him. Marina pushed all thoughts of the mission and her uncertain future away, concentrating instead on the sound of Kaden's strong heartbeat and the way he held her as if he never wanted to let her go.

Chapter Eleven

Kaden fought the urge to press Marina against the nearest smooth *banlah* tree and fuck her senseless. Unfortunately, he had to concentrate on their mission. "Tonight, we will approach Zim with our plan. We'll explain that you are so happy in your new role that you want to bring other women to Xarta, and I'll subtly suggest that I'd like to assist him."

"Won't he suspect we know what's going on? These women are supposed to be willing."

"I know Zim. His thoughts will be so filled with money he won't even consider it. Besides, our suggestion will be innocent. You obviously know you weren't brought here willingly, and he'll know that, too. But you've been 'transformed', so to speak. Don't worry about it."

Marina looked over at him, her green eyes sparkling like the emeralds at her breasts. The pink light made her face glow a brilliant bronze. When she smiled at him, his heart stopped. "Think I can pull that off?"

He frowned. "Pull what off?"

"Telling Zim that I'm ecstatically happy being a slave."

Kaden masked his disappointment at Marina's words. "Depends on how good an actress you are."

Her lips curled in a smile that made his balls ache. "Oh, I can be very persuasive."

And soon, he'd see how persuasive *he* could be. After the mission, he intended to keep Marina with him, no matter what. But right now a promise glimmered in her eyes. Seductive, tantalizing, and he wanted more. "Persuasive, are you? Show me."

They were walking through the palace gardens, a place where they were not monitored. Kaden stepped back into a private area surrounded by dense trees and tall bushes. He leaned against a *banlah* tree, waiting for her. Marina followed him, a devilish glint in her eyes. His cock was already hard thinking of how Marina might "persuade" him.

Her body was lush, her assets barely concealed by the sheer dress. Her skin was a golden sun on its own, casting a crystal light around her. She stepped into the shade and dropped her gaze to the ground, stopping no more than a finger's breadth away.

"May I touch you, Sire?" she asked, adopting the formal tone of a sub, a fact that greatly pleased him.

"Yes."

"And kiss you, Sire?"

"Yes, get on with it."

He saw her lips curl into a smile. "Anything I want to do to you, Sire?"

Frustration welled within him. He could smell her, the sweet flowery perfume from the bathing pool coupled with her own unique scent more than a little distracting. "Yes, dammit. Hurry."

She looked up at him then, fire burning in her gaze. Her sweet breath sailed across his cheek as she leaned into him and wound her arms around his waist, then pressed her lips against his.

Kaden tensed at the first touch of her tongue along his lips, then groaned when she slid her tongue inside his mouth, seeking his. He crushed her against his chest and kissed her deeply, with a longing that shocked him. His body nearly shook with desire for her and he was already desperate to plunge into her moist, heated cunt.

She palmed his cock through his pants, and he knew then that there would be no time with foreplay. He took her mouth in a heated kiss while she hurriedly opened his pants. Desperate to feel her surrounding him, he yanked her dress up over her buttocks, raised her leg over his hip and drove into her creamy pussy with one quick thrust.

Marina cried out and hooked her leg tighter against him, grinding her sex against his inflamed shaft. She was so hot, so tight, that his balls drew up against his body, already prepared to release. Her cunt squeezed him, milking him, urging him to finish. Her nails scraped over his shoulders and arms as she thrust furiously against him. He watched the passion rise on her face, the intense look in her emerald eyes, the way she gripped him so tight, pulsing around him. Her responses drove him mad. He couldn't hold back any longer, needing to release inside her.

"Come, Marina. Now."

A scream tore from her throat and she climaxed, tossing her head back and riding him hard and fast. Her pussy gripped him and pulsed over and over again, taking him with her.

When he could once again manage words, he kissed her gently, smiling down at her. "That was quite persuasive."

A blush of satisfaction tinged her cheeks. "I'm glad you thought so, Sire."

"Let's go get ready for tonight. We have a big evening ahead of us."

She nodded and he led her down the path toward the palace, wondering if they would be able to find the missing women tonight and, more importantly, resolve the issue of those responsible for the slave trading ring.

If so, his time with Marina was limited, something he hadn't wanted to think about, but knew was coming. He still couldn't read her emotions. Yes, he knew when she was aroused, and she seemed to take quite well to being submissive, at least sexually. But would she want to adopt this lifestyle after their mission was over?

They did, after all, lead completely separate lives. She had a career on Earth, and his consisted of traveling the galaxies. Not quite conducive to a Dom and sub relationship, was it?

One of them would have to give in order to make it work. And since he couldn't figure out whether she was even interested in continuing their relationship, he supposed he'd better determine that first, and work out the rest later.

* * * * *

Marina stared at her reflection in the full-length mirror of the bathroom, finding it hard to believe that the woman staring back was her.

For someone who'd always worn pants, non-flattering ones at that, the new Marina was quite a shock.

Her face was flushed from hours spent making love with Kaden, her hair a wild curling mass. Every curve of her body was outlined beneath the see-through golden gown, her large breasts nearly falling out of the low-cut bodice.

She'd never been one to admire her own body, always feeling as if she was a bit on the large side, with too-full hips and too-muscular thighs. But outfitted like this, she was all woman. Voluptuous, desirable, the kind of woman a man might actually want.

A man like Kaden, perhaps?

She peeked around the corner, watching him put on his suede pants and matching sleeveless tunic. The material shaped itself to his finely sculpted ass, and she wished she could spend the evening with her hands attached to those globes of firm flesh. Instead, they had to play out this game to its hopefully positive conclusion.

Still, she couldn't help but take one last glance at the woman in the mirror, a woman whose face glowed with a radiance that could only be described as love.

There were so many questions she wanted to ask Kaden, so many things she wanted to tell him about how she felt.

But those things would have to wait until all this was over, until she had a chance to get a clearer indication of where his heart was, of how he really felt about her.

Until then, she'd do her job.

She stepped out of the bathroom and he turned to her, his gaze heating like a spark igniting an inferno. Heat flushed her slit and she felt the now-familiar moisture gathering. Her breasts tingled, the charms at her nipples vibrating under his assessment.

Kaden walked toward her, took her hand in his and pressed his lips to her knuckles. "You are truly beautiful," he said.

She believed him. "Thank you, Sire."

"Keep in mind all that you have learned of your required obedience this evening, as this is my opportunity to show you off."

She nodded, and followed him through the open doorway toward the ballroom. Tonight, she wanted to please him, wanted him to see that she could adapt, had already adapted to being his sub. She wore his jewels with pride, and for the first time in her life, entered a room confident, self-assured and damned happy to be tethered to a man like Kaden.

He belonged to her, and she wasn't going to let him go.

All eyes turned to them as they entered. Sucking in a huge breath of courage, she followed submissively behind Kaden as they entered the expansive room already filled with people.

Not too different from a party on Earth. Fancy decorations on the tables, music playing from a live band on the stage, and people milling about eating, drinking and talking. They even had a dance floor!

Kaden nodded to several men as they passed. Marina made sure to keep her gaze lowered, but still managed to catch a glimpse of the people they walked by.

"Marina, raise your head."

She did, and looked into his smiling face.

"You may view the festivities tonight, you may speak freely, but only to me and to other women, not to any of the men unless I give you permission."

Was that a standard rule, or was he merely being possessive of her? She hoped it was the latter. "Yes, Sire."

They milled about for awhile, eating and drinking the strange concoctions she'd developed a taste for. Their drinks and meals were all based from their own agricultural stores of grains, fruits and vegetables, and Marina had quickly adapted to their sweet flavors.

"Come, dance with me," Kaden said, pulling her onto the dance floor.

The band played a slow, seductive song, using instruments she'd never seen before. The tunes were similar to soft, sexy love songs, and Marina found herself deeply into the mournful strains as she rested her head against Kaden's chest. She inhaled his masculine fragrance, memorizing his scent as one she would never forget.

Quit thinking that this is the last night he's going to hold you in his arms. She fought the melancholy and concentrated instead on searching the ballroom for anyone who looked remotely familiar.

Telor and Rora stood beside the dance floor, and she smiled at the blonde as they passed by. She wondered if Rora was involved in the slave trade because she wanted to be, or because she didn't have any other choice. As her gaze traveled over the other dancers, she tensed and blinked, recognizing a tall brunette as one of the kidnapped women. She reached up and pulled Kaden to her for a kiss, then whispered, "I see one of the women."

His gaze followed hers and he nodded. "Keep looking. I think I saw one, too."

Hope burst within her. She wanted nothing more than to rescue the women who had been taken against their will, unable to comprehend the horror and worry their families had experienced in the months they'd been missing. If they could return them to Earth, the mission would be successful. If they could shut down the portal and the slave trade, it would be more than she could have hoped for.

"Let's see what we can find out," he said, maneuvering them toward the tall brunette who was dancing with her eyes closed, her head resting on her Dom's shoulder.

"Greetings," Kaden said to the fat Zartelian. Tall, he was also extremely wide, his face covered with a yellow pall that made him look like he was ill. He was also very sweaty.

Marina swallowed, grateful to be with Kaden in more ways than one.

"Well, hello," the Zartelian said, his gaze trained on Marina. She kept her gaze on the floor, not wanting to show the man her revulsion at his appearance. She supposed on Zartel, he'd be considered attractive.

"Your female is very beautiful," Kaden said, motioning to the brunette who now stared submissively at the floor. "May I have a dance with her?"

The Zartelian licked his lips, a bit of drool seeping out of the corner of his mouth. Marina shuddered, and Kaden tightened his grip reassuringly.

"I'd be delighted. This is my sub, Louisa, and I am Mok."

"Greetings, Mok. I am Kaden and this is my sub, Marina."

Kaden gave her hand a squeeze and moved her toward Mok. She'd do what she had to do so Kaden could speak with Louisa, but damn this wasn't going to be fun.

Mok wrapped his thick arms around her and pulled her close to his chest. For once she was grateful for her submissive posture, so he wouldn't see the distaste in her eyes.

"You are one handful of woman," Mok said, rocking what she supposed was his cock against her upper thigh and squeezing her buttocks with both hands.

"You are too kind, Sire," she said, searching the dance floor for Kaden. She found him, his head bent toward the brunette's ear. His arms were wrapped tightly around Louisa, and she smiled when he said something to her.

She hoped the woman was smiling because Kaden had just informed her who they were and what they were going to do.

He'd mentioned when she first arrived that he'd fuck one of the missing women if necessary to get close enough to speak with one.

Marina hoped that wouldn't be necessary.

"You are an Earth woman," Mok said.

"Yes, Sire."

"And how do you like being a submissive?"

"I am enjoying it very much, Sire."

"Yes, I'm sure Kaden keeps that sweet pussy of yours filled regularly, doesn't he?"

She refused to answer, considering it wasn't any of his business.

"I might wish to fuck you myself, Marina. Or perhaps Kaden and I could fuck you together while Louisa pleasured you. Would you enjoy that, my sweet?"

Not in this lifetime, or any other. "Yes, Sire." She tried not to gag as she spoke the words.

"Perhaps I'll mention this to Kaden."

The music ended and Kaden brought Louisa back to Mok. Bowing his head, he said, "It was a great honor to be allowed to dance with Louisa, Mok. Many thanks."

"You are most welcome," Mok said. "I had a very enjoyable conversation with Marina. I will be speaking to you later about the possibility of fucking her."

Kaden had been slipping his arms around Marina's waist when Mok spoke of having her. He went still, his fingers curled into the small of her back and his body tensed.

So, he didn't want Mok to fuck her. She fought back a smile.

"Yes, we will speak later." Quickly maneuvering Marina away, he took her outside the palace for a walk.

When they were out of earshot, he said, "Enjoy your dance?"

"No, Sire. I did not."

Her honesty seemed to satisfy him. "Good. What a slovenly, fat fucker. I'll be damned if I let another man touch you."

She couldn't help her smile and squeezed his hand tight, beaming inside and out. Perhaps he did care for her after all.

"Louisa admitted to being kidnapped, and obviously she's more than a little relieved at the thought of being rescued from Mok."

Marina snorted. "I don't doubt that, Sire. He's quite...revolting."

"She's also made contact with one of the other women from Earth, who is still here at the palace. That woman wants to be freed, also, and admits to being kidnapped."

"We must hurry then, Sire."

He nodded. "I agree. The sooner the better. But they're both well, and their Doms do not mistreat them. Louisa does not want to stay here a moment longer than she has to."

"I'm glad we found her, Sire. Let's hope we can get her home soon."

"It's time," he whispered. "Let's go put on a little show for Zim."

She nodded and Kaden led her toward the slave master.

Zim was dressed in fancy robes, beaming as if he expected personal gratitude for bringing in the new crop of slave women. He grinned as Kaden approached.

"Good evening, Kaden. I trust you are satisfied with your purchase?"

Marina fought the shudder as Zim's gaze raked over her body.

"Indeed, I am. Marina has taken quite well to the lifestyle here. She is much more than I could have hoped for. You did well in meeting my needs."

Zim continued to watch her. Marina stayed in her submissive stance, head bowed.

"Yes, there was quite a bidding war over her. I wish we had many more like her."

"As a matter of fact, I have a proposition for you, if you're interested."

Marina could imagine Zim nearly drooling over Kaden's statement.

"What kind of proposition?"

"May we have a moment of privacy with you?"

"Of course. Come with me to my offices."

Zim could smell money and a deal. Marina was certain of it. He practically ran toward his offices, hurriedly closing the door behind them and motioning them to sit.

"Now. What kind of proposition do you have in mind?"

Kaden motioned to Marina. "My submissive has grown to love it here on Xarta, as well as the lifestyle. She has offered to alert whoever brought her here to other potentials from Earth."

Marina wished she could read Zim's expression.

"You may raise your head and look at Zim, Marina," Kaden commanded.

"Yes, Sire." She lifted her gaze to Zim's and nodded at him. "Master Zim."

He pursed his lips. "Marina. If possible, you are lovelier now than when you first came to us."

She bowed her head. "Thank you, Master Zim. I am honored by your words."

Zim nodded. "What makes you think that we wish to bring other women here?"

Kaden grinned. "I know how much I paid for Marina. If there are others like her, you stand to make quite a sum."

The slave master steepled his fingers. "Very true. What's in it for you, Kaden?"

Kaden settled back in the chair and draped his arm over Marina's shoulders. "A cut of your profits, of course. I plan to stay on Xarta now that I have Marina." He caressed her cheek with the back of his hand. "My traveling days are behind me."

"Excellent," Zim said. "I'm pleased you are taking me up on my long-ago offer. I thought several years ago that you were going to take my head off when I suggested you and I work together. Now, we are honored that one of our own is coming home to stay."

"Thank you. Several years ago, I didn't really know what I wanted. I just knew I needed to get out and explore other galaxies. Now that I'm back on my home planet, with an excellent slave such as Marina, I am anxious to get started on a joint venture with you. I find that I will need an income, though. And since Marina has been so desirous of bringing her own people here, this could be a winning situation for both of us."

Well that explained how Kaden could get their idea across so convincingly. Zim had already wanted him to take part in the slave trade.

"Very true. But how do I know I can trust you?" Zim asked.

Kaden crossed his arms and arched a brow. "You mean because women like Marina are not brought here of their own accord? That, in fact, they are kidnapped?"

Zim paled, if it were possible for him to blanch any further than his natural white pallor.

Kaden waved his hand. "Relax, Zim. If I wanted to turn you in, I'd have done so by now. I believe what you and your partners have here is quite a lucrative business. Since Marina can supply us with women, we can quickly make a lot of money, I think we can strike a deal that would be mutually beneficial."

"You make a very tempting offer, Kaden." His gaze turned to Marina. "How many women are we talking about?"

Marina looked at Kaden, who nodded. "At least a dozen that I can think of, Master Zim. Possibly more." To add emphasis, she asked, "Master Zim, may I add to my statement?"

He nodded. "Go on."

"There are a lot of lonely women on Earth. Many are friends of mine, who haven't been able to find the right man. Before I came here I didn't even know what I wanted. I would never have thought myself submissive." She turned to Kaden and showed him the honest emotion she felt in her heart. His eyes widened and she looked again at Zim. "But now that I'm here, I know my friends could be equally as happy, Master."

"I see."

She read the dollar signs in Zim's dark eyes and knew they had him.

"How quickly can we begin?" Zim asked.

Got him! Now it was up to Kaden to set the trap.

"Immediately. After you tell me who else is involved and how the transportation is handled. Marina and I will handle things on the Earth side."

Zim regarded Kaden for a few minutes, as if he pondered whether or not Kaden could be trusted. Finally, he nodded. "Very well. Telor is our contact on Earth. Others handle the various galaxies. He'll be happy to move somewhere else, though, since he's not fond of the Earth planet any longer. We were afraid the portal would have to be moved."

So they were right! It *was* a portal rather than a transport ship. That explained her lack of vertigo when she woke.

"Where is the portal now?"

"We can move it within a several click radius of a few clubs in one of the major cities in your North America," he said to Marina. "Once we finish there, it can be closed up and relocated somewhere on another planet. There are only a few locations on Earth where it was stable enough to be used. San Francisco was one of them."

She nodded.

"Can you lure the women to a specified location?" he asked her.

"Yes, Master Zim." What a sick, greedy bastard he was. Dealing in human flesh as if these women were not individuals with minds and choices of their own. She fought to keep the loathing from showing on her face.

"So, we begin tonight?" Kaden asked.

"Yes, if you're willing. The sooner the better. After the excitement over Marina, I want to strike while we have enthusiastic buyers still in attendance. I will guide you the first time and fill you in on how it's done. After that, you will be able to handle the tasks alone."

"Very well. We'll come back after the party is over."

"Excellent!" Zim rubbed his hands together while Marina fought back the bile rising to her throat. She hoped she'd have an opportunity to see him rot in Earth's prison.

Kaden negotiated payment, percentages of profit and other matters, then they left Zim's office and went back to the party, acting as if nothing had happened. Marina stayed close to Kaden while trying to spot more of the kidnapped women. By the time the evening had wound down, they had identified at least three, but unfortunately didn't get a chance to talk to any of them. Their sires guarded them too closely, and unless either Kaden or Marina could get the women alone, the opportunity to obtain any information was lost. But at least they knew the women were alive. Kaden whispered to her that he would identify the Doms and their current locations and they could get to the women after they closed the portal. It was important not to call too much attention to themselves now that they'd played their hand with Zim. Seeking out the kidnapped Earth women would surely have alerted him to their plot.

Kaden led them back to their room before the party ended, drawing Marina into his arms before the door had even fully shut. His lips covered hers, his tongue diving inside and searching deeply for her response.

A response she was all too eager to give. She kissed him with a desperate passion, realizing this could very well be the last time. Now was not the time for games of submission and dominance. She knew exactly what she wanted, and she was going to have to ask him for it.

She whimpered, desperately needing to speak.

"Say what's on your mind, Marina."

"Sire," she whispered breathlessly. "Make love to me, please."

He'd left the lights off, but she felt his shuddering breath as his mouth once again descended on hers. Clothes were discarded like the slide of silken sheets along soft flesh. They fell into bed, caressing each other's bodies and whispering heated words of passion.

Kaden rolled Marina onto her back and spread her legs, reaching for her swollen slit to test her readiness. He needn't have bothered. She'd been wet from the moment his lips had touched hers. "Are you ready for me, Marina?"

"Yes, Sire. Oh, yes. Please, Sire, hurry."

He situated himself between her legs and drove into her with one quick thrust. She cried out and wrapped her legs around his waist, pulling him deeply inside her.

They moved against one another, taking, giving, caught in an emotional moment where no words were necessary, only the silent cries of passion and the touch of mouths to skin.

Marina fought the tears, refusing to acknowledge this would be the last time she'd hold Kaden close to her. Instead, she focused on the driving thrusts of his cock as he took her to peak after peak of sensational orgasms. She came hard and fast each time, emotion mingling with passion as she poured out her love to him in the only way she could.

Kaden finally joined her, roaring out loud as he climaxed within her.

They lay there for a few quiet moments, stroking and kissing each other. Then, Kaden withdrew, mumbling about needing to dress so they could meet Zim.

A sudden chill surrounded her as she lost the warmth of his body around hers, and she felt a loneliness that she hadn't felt since before she met him.

A loneliness she never wanted to feel again.

Chapter Twelve

Marina and Kaden arrived at Zim's offices, dressed in appropriate Earth clothing. Marina was once again dressed in what she must have been wearing when she arrived, a short miniskirt and tight-fitting top. Zim smiled when they walked in. Well, he leered at Marina, and smiled politely at Kaden.

Kaden made a mental note that at some point, Zim would have a fist in his mouth for the way he ogled Marina.

His reactions to other men around Marina had seemed more and more like jealousy with each day that passed. Very unlike him to worry about other men looking at his sub, yet with Marina it was decidedly different.

He knew why, hadn't wanted to lend voice to his thoughts, and now was not the time. Later there'd be time for self-examination and decisions. Now, he needed to close this portal and put an end to the slave ring.

"I see you're right on time," Zim said. "Shall we get started?"

He led them through the hallways to the preparation rooms where Marina had been taken after her arrival on Xarta. Behind the tables was a hidden door, made visible with the wave of Zim's hand. Zim opened it and led them down a dark hallway toward a small shimmering light.

"The portal?" Kaden asked.

"Yes. We must hold hands and enter together. Otherwise we could be separated."

"Why?"

"The portal moves a bit each time, so you don't arrive in exactly the same spot. If we go through separately, we could be lost."

Great. An unstable portal. He grabbed Zim's and Marina's hands and Zim led the way into the mass of shimmering waves.

Instantly, they were standing in an alleyway on Earth. He looked to Marina to be sure she was okay, and she nodded.

"Not too far from one of the nightclubs," Zim said.

It was evening and fog slithered around them. A chill filled the air and Kaden drew his coat tighter around him. The fog was like a cloak over all sounds, lending a quiet eeriness to the location.

"If the portal moves each time, do you doubt its stability?" Kaden asked.

"No, no, it's stable. It just hovers within a few clicks, location-wise. Trust me, we haven't lost anyone yet."

"Good. I'd hate to be stuck on Earth with an unwilling captive and no way back to Xarta."

Zim laughed. "No fear of that. We have people on this side who help us, so even if the portal wasn't locatable for a short period of time, there are those who would hide you."

And those were the people he and Marina needed to uncover, to put an end to the entire ring of slavers. At least on Earth. Then he could start working on the other galaxies.

"I'll need to meet those contacts, then. I want to be covered in case something happens."

Zim nodded. "Of course. But you needn't worry. I can recall the portal at any time."

He lifted the sleeve of his shirt to reveal something glowing under the skin of his inner wrist. "This is the controller to the portal. I can move it, delete it, or recall it at any time with the simple touch of a button. This is also a defense weapon in case of attack."

Not good. If Zim had weaponry embedded in his skin, he'd be difficult to take down.

"Let's go meet our contact," Zim said, leading them down the alley to the back door of a club.

Kaden reached into his coat pocket for his combination tazer/laser, feeling comforted that if he had to, he could take Zim out before he had a chance to do anything to the portal or to Marina. They stepped into the club and were immediately greeted by a burly looking guard. He nodded and allowed them to pass. Kaden memorized the guard's face since he obviously knew Zim.

Zim introduced them to the man behind the bar, informing them he was the owner of the club. His name was Lars, and Zim informed them that Lars also owned the other three clubs where the girls were taken from.

That was a revelation. No one knew Lars owned all of the clubs. He must have put the other two in another name so there'd be no way to connect him to the kidnappings from all the clubs he owned. Perhaps he had multiple businesses under various names, and was able to hide his identity. Kaden would do a little research on that as soon as this was over. He didn't want any strings left hanging.

Kaden had no intention of doing anything to Lars or the guard tonight. Right now he wanted to get that controller from Zim, and had to figure out a way to do that. Once Zim was neutralized, they could come back and deal with the others.

"Tonight we'll just look around," Zim said, nearly shouting to be heard over the blaring music. "Get you familiar with how this works. Lars will be your contact point here, along with the man at the door, Tiny."

Marina swallowed a laugh. Tiny? That seven foot hulking monster who guarded the back door was named Tiny?

"Marina. You will dance with me," Zim said.

Marina turned to Kaden, who didn't look at all pleased with Zim's suggestion.

"I don't think so," Kaden responded.

Zim shook his head. "You misunderstand, my friend. It wouldn't do at all for you to be seen dancing only with her. The best way to get women to agree to go outside with you is to have them start seeing you here alone. Go ask someone to dance. It's good for business."

Marina read the murderous look in Kaden's eyes, feeling somewhat comforted by the fact he didn't want another man touching her. But he finally nodded and Zim dragged her onto the dance floor.

It would have to be a slow song that started up, requiring Zim to pull her close. Nausea rose as she felt his erection pressing up against her mound. The man made her sick.

"Someday, Marina, I would very much like to fuck you."

Someday, Zim, I will squeeze your balls so hard you'll scream like a girl. "I am honored, Master Zim," she said, choking the words out.

He rocked against her, and she had no choice but to endure his blatant sexual advances. "I'm sure I could convince Kaden that I could make it worthwhile. Besides, part of your duties as a slave is to serve all masters."

"Yes, Master Zim."

Didn't any of the Doms practice monogamy? Well, Kaden did, at least so far. He hadn't once wanted to touch another woman. Was it that he was truly satisfied with her, or was he just staying close to her because he was doing his job?

Some questions had no answers, and she had no time to search for them now.

She bowed her head, grateful not to have to look Zim in the eye. Surely he'd be able to read her hatred in them. She looked for Kaden, who was leaning against the bar talking to a gorgeous redhead. Jealousy filled her and she fought it back. This was a job. She was doing hers, and he was doing his.

Besides, after this mission was over, she'd have no claim on Kaden. Hell, for that matter, she had no claim on him now. He'd never once led her to believe that he wanted to have anything to do with her after their job was finished.

The dance seemed to go on forever. Finally, it ended and Zim returned her to the bar. He warned her to steer clear of Kaden, who was occupied talking and laughing with the redhead. Putting her brain into work mode, she turned to Lars, who smiled at her and offered her a drink.

She asked for water, not trusting any sweet-tasting drinks a stranger offered ever again.

The night wore on and Marina grew more and more irritated at having to stand by and do nothing but fend off the men in the bar who came up and asked her to dance. Lars and Zim spoke in hushed whispers at the other end of the bar. Kaden remained with the redhead, dancing and laughing and buying her drinks while Marina steamed, mentally plotting ways to slice off his dick and hiding it where he'd never find it again.

Jealousy wasn't very becoming on her, she decided, reminding herself that this was all an act, including what Kaden was doing with the redhead. When the redhead left for the bathroom, Kaden approached the bar, motioning to Zim.

"She wants to go with me," he said.

"Excellent!" Zim announced. "Marina, you and I will go outside and wait for Kaden. Tiny will make sure no one else comes out after Kaden and the woman. Then we will open the portal and leave. See how simple all this is?"

She was counting the minutes until they could turn the tables on Zim. When Zim went to tell Lars the plan, Kaden quickly leaned over and whispered to her.

"When we get outside, I'll take Zim down. I need you to distract him first, so that I can get to the controller embedded in his arm. You know what you need to do."

"Of course." As much as it sickened her, she knew exactly what would capture Zim's attention.

"Good. Follow my lead. We have enough to bring them all in now."

She nodded, eager to get into action.

Kaden quickly moved back to his position at the bar, and Zim led Marina outside and down the alley. He lifted his sleeve and pressed a green button glowing inside his wrist. "The portal is prepared. We just have to wait for Kaden and the woman. Lars will have put the drug in her drink, so she should be getting very woozy right now."

Marina remembered the feeling.

Now it was her turn to keep him occupied. "Master Zim, may I speak?"

"Yes."

She crept closer, winding her arm around his neck. "I know this is improper of me, but I couldn't help but be aroused at your suggestion earlier."

Zim's eyes darkened. "You want me."

In your dreams, dickhead. She lowered her eyes and grit her teeth. "Yes, Master Zim. I'm sorry, but I felt compelled to tell you. Please do not punish me."

Zim lifted her chin. "You will not be punished. At least not right now. You make my cock hard for you, Marina. I want you to suck it."

She feigned wide-eyed fear. "But my sire—"

"You don't need to worry about Kaden. He will share you. Why, it will excite him to see you on your knees sucking me. Wouldn't you like to arouse him?"

"Very much, Master Zim." Ugh. She might barf if she had to speak in such a subservient tone for much longer.

"Then suck me. Now."

She dropped to her knees, palming his shaft and fighting back the shudders that threatened to reveal her utter revulsion. Turning Zim so that his back was to the alleyway, she slowly unzipped his pants, reaching for his cock and grasping it firmly in her hands.

Ick. This whole scenario was disgusting. But if it saved Kaden and put an end to the portal and slave trade, she'd do whatever was necessary.

Zim groaned and closed his eyes. Perfect, since she spotted Kaden approaching, carrying the unconscious redhead in his arms.

She kept her eyes on Kaden as she yanked Zim's pants to his knees and began to stroke his cock in earnest.

"Suck me woman. If I don't have your mouth around me soon I'll explode."

Oh, he was going to explode all right. But not in the way he wanted. Kaden laid the woman gently on the ground, then crept toward Zim, a murderous expression on his face.

Whatever Kaden intended for Zim, it wasn't going to be good. She hoped he'd bash Zim's head in. In fact, she'd like to do the honors, but her position didn't give her much of an advantage. At least not toward the head attached to his neck.

Zim hadn't heard Kaden's approach. He was so focused on her attentions to his shaft that he probably wouldn't notice a bomb exploding nearby. Kaden was only inches away now. She licked her lips, drawing her mouth closer to the head of Zim's cock. Just one more second and—

Zim must have heard Kaden, because he whipped around and quickly pushed a button on his arm just as Kaden was about to hit him with the tazer. A sharp green blast emanated from Zim's wrist, striking Kaden in the chest.

Kaden dropped to a heap on the ground.

Fear filled her. She had to think, quickly. Her first instinct was to run to Kaden and see if he was all right, but she knew she had to subdue Zim first. With him out of action, she could get to Kaden.

She quickly bent over and laid her head on the ground, feigning a wailing cry. "Master Zim! Please do not blame me for this. I knew nothing of what my sire planned!"

She made numerous whimpering noises until Zim lifted her by the hair. "Shut up woman, or you'll draw a crowd!"

He looked at Kaden, who remained motionless on the ground, then further down the alley where the redhead lie unconscious. Turning back to her, he smiled. "It is time for us to go, but not until I get what you promised me. Hurry, bitch. Suck me and make me come."

His cock was still erect. The bastard.

Which gave her the perfect opportunity to do exactly what she'd wanted. "Yes, Master Zim. Thank you so much."

"Do it and quit talking!" He slapped her hard across the face. Sonofabitch, that stung! Real tears sprang to her eyes and she had to shake her head to regain her focus. She grasped Zim's still hard cock…the prick obviously got off on hurting women. She stroked him, drawing ever closer with her mouth, then reached underneath and caressed his balls with her fingers, eliciting a loud groan from him. Capturing his gaze in hers, she mesmerized him by licking her lips, darting her tongue out so that it was only a fraction of an inch from his swollen cock.

His eyes glazed over in passion and he tangled his fingers in her hair, pulling her closer to him. She took that moment to grasp both his balls and squeeze them like she was drawing juice from a lemon, digging her fingernails into the soft sacs.

Zim squealed in a high-pitched tone and dropped to his knees, taking her with him. Dammit, her hair was wound in his fingers and she couldn't get free! She struggled to move him, but he was just too damn big. Finally she tugged hard, viciously pulling at her own hair until she whimpered with the pain.

On her knees, she struck at him, leveling a punch to his nose that sent blood flying everywhere.

Fury boiled in his eyes and he lunged for her. She stood and kicked his ribs, then planted her foot on his windpipe. Zim gagged, but grabbed her foot and wrenched it sideways.

Marina heard the sickening pop and leaped away, limping. Zim stood and took off after her. The throbbing in her ankle kept her from running at her usual speed, but she hoped he was too injured to give a quick chase.

She wasn't fast enough. Zim caught up to her, whirled her around and grabbed her by the throat. Despite having to hold her weight on her injured ankle, she leveled a kick at his chin, catching the side of his jaw before he backed out of the way. He grabbed her swollen, throbbing foot and tossed her to the ground.

The wind temporarily knocked out of her, she was helpless to move. Zim descended on her stomach, punched her in the face, then reached for her throat, cutting off her windpipe. Marina fought to remain conscious after the brutal blows, but the sick pounding in her temple nearly caused her to lose it.

"Traitorous bitch! You'll die for this."

Hot pain surrounded her, the choking sensation unbearable. She grabbed for his hand, trying desperately to pull it free of her throat, but he was too strong for her. He scooted forward onto her chest, further cutting off her ability to fight him.

She was going to die. As white spots appeared in front of her eyes, she realized she would die at the hands of this sick vermin.

But then his fingers relaxed. Marina coughed and wheezed, sucking in air. She reached for his wrist to pull him away from her throat, horrified when she realized that his hand and wrist were no longer attached to his body. She quickly threw the unattached limb to the ground and looked up to see Kaden standing over her with a laser device in his hand.

The weapon had sliced Zim's arm from his body. She turned to see Zim crumpled to the ground, holding the stump of his arm and writhing in shock and pain. She felt no sympathy for him.

Kaden slipped the device in his pocket and reached for Zim's severed hand, tucking it into his other pocket. He gently pulled her up and lifted her into his arms. Marina swayed and fought off the dizziness, but one eye was already swollen shut from the beating Zim had given her, and her throat was so raw she couldn't speak.

She tried to open her mouth to say something, but no words came out, only a searing pain from the attempt. Her throat felt like it was ten times the normal size and her ankle throbbed incessantly.

"Shhh, *zejehr*, don't speak. We have the device and I've notified your authorities, who are on their way to arrest Lars and Tiny. We can close the portal and then I'll deal with Telor later. We need to get you to a medical facility."

She shook her head, not wanting to go to a hospital. She wanted to go home, and managed to croak the single word.

Kaden shook his head. "Hospital first."

The sound of sirens drew closer, and Marina knew she didn't have the strength to argue with him. She laid her head on his chest and gave up, letting the blissful darkness overtake her.

When she woke, she was in the emergency room, where the doctors quickly checked her out and applied bandages to the cuts on her face. She was bruised, badly, but her windpipe was sound. The doctors told her not to speak for the next few days. Her ankle was sprained and swollen, but no break and no ligament damage, fortunately. She should be able to walk on it once the swelling went down.

Kaden stayed with her, talking via communicator with Laren and the authorities. Lars and Tiny had been taken into custody and the portal codes had been deciphered and closed. Marina drifted in and out of consciousness, trying to fight the effects of the painkillers they had given her.

Finally, the doctor released her and Kaden took her home. He treated her so tenderly, first bathing her and washing the dirt stains from her body, then tucking her into bed with a glass of warm liquid that soothed her raw throat.

Every time she tried to say something, he glared at her and warned her not to talk.

How could she not speak? She had so much to say to him. Questions to ask, to feel him out, see how he felt about the two of them now that their mission was over. At least the part of the mission that required them to be together.

Or maybe he'd bring it up and she wouldn't have to.

"You get some rest, and no talking," he said, pulling the covers up to her chin. "I'm heading out to tie up some loose ends and file my report. I'll see you tomorrow."

He kissed her on the forehead and shut out the light. In a few seconds, she heard the door to her apartment close.

A kiss on the forehead.

After all they'd been through together, he gave her a kiss on the forehead.

That didn't bode well for their future, did it?

* * * * *

Kaden stormed out the door and jumped into his vehicle, slamming the door and taking off much faster than he should have.

Dammit, she looked way too vulnerable lying there in her bed, her face all bruised and swollen, purple handprints around her neck.

Fury still boiled within him, so much that he wanted to search out Zim and show him what strangulation really felt like.

He'd also wanted to stay with her, crawl into bed with her, hold her tight and swear that he'd never let anyone hurt her again.

But he knew she'd hate that. Strong, independent Marina wouldn't stand for a man who wanted to protect her, to dominate her in every way possible, including her safety. She had too much pride in her job and self-sufficiency to ever want a man like that.

Problem was, he *was* that man.

The wrong man for a woman like her.

What he was going to do with that knowledge, he wasn't certain. It sure changed his thoughts about what would happen between them, though. Now that she was back on Earth, he realized that he'd been wrong in thinking he could just tell her the way things would be between them. What they'd had on Xarta was a game, not reality. And he'd fallen under a spell of dominance and submission, thinking Marina had really accepted his lifestyle.

But she hadn't, and she never would. Marina was a dominant woman who would never be happy taking a submissive role. She was strong, capable, and able to take care of herself. Except tonight, with Zim. And only because Kaden had put her in that position in the first place, assuming she'd act like a true submissive, not as the strong enforcer that she was.

His mistake had almost cost her life, and he wouldn't make an error in judgment like that again.

She'd be much better off when he was out of her life for good.

Chapter Thirteen

Two days later Marina was back in the office, her voice nearly restored and the swelling gone down enough that she didn't quite resemble Quasimodo any longer.

Besides, she was tired of staring at the walls in her apartment, wondering what Kaden was doing.

He hadn't been back to see her since the night he'd tucked her in and placed a brotherly kiss on her forehead. That night he'd told her he'd see her the next day. She'd waited, but he hadn't shown up. Nor had he called.

Which only made her worry and conjure up all kinds of things in her mind. Things she shouldn't be thinking about.

Time to focus on work instead of on Kaden. She headed to Laren's office for her debriefing, knocking lightly.

The door slid open, as did her mouth when she saw who was in there.

Kaden.

Dressed all in black, his blond hair sticking out like he'd just gotten out of a wild wind. Just the way she loved him.

Wild.

She loved him. She was pissed as hell that he hadn't come back, and yet so damn glad to see him again she could drop to the floor and sob. God, what was she going to do?

"How are you feeling?" Laren asked.

"Great. Fit and ready for work."

Laren laughed. "That's so typical. You're still bruised and battered, Marina. You'll be doing paperwork for awhile longer."

"I'm fine, really," she said to Laren, but she couldn't take her focus away from Kaden. She'd missed him. Her heart felt like someone had clenched it in their fist. Just the sight of him brought her to near tears. What the hell was wrong with her, anyway?

"You look fine," Kaden said, neither smiling nor frowning at her.

"Thanks."

"Uh, I have a meeting to attend. Kaden, please fill Marina in on the past couple days' happenings while I'm gone."

Kaden nodded and Laren stopped in front of Marina, a worried expression on her face. "I'm glad you're okay. Welcome back."

"Thanks."

Laren left and the door shut behind her. Kaden motioned Marina to sit in the chair across from him.

"Zim is in the holding cell awaiting transport back to Xarta. Your judicial system will take care of Lars and Tiny. The portal has been closed, and Telor has been detained on Xarta awaiting my return."

"Sounds like you have things wrapped up then."

"Yes. I'm sure you're glad this is over. Now you don't have to fake being a submissive any longer."

What did he mean by that? That he was glad he didn't have to deal with her any longer? "Yes, it's nice to get back home again and resume my normal life." *My normal, boring, routine, no excitement existence.*

Kaden frowned. "Yes, I'm sure you're happy that you don't have to deal with being something you're not."

She wasn't a submissive, was what he meant. He'd never thought she could be one, and despite the great sex they had, he didn't see her as one now. Because she'd failed him as a submissive. Despite what she'd thought they'd shared on Xarta, she'd been nothing more than a duty to him, an act to ensnare Zim and the others.

Marina sighed, not knowing what else to say to him. She'd never tell him her feelings now. He'd laugh at her. "When do you leave?"

He paused before speaking. "Tonight. We closed the portal so I'm taking a transport ship back to Xarta."

"I see. Looks like I'll be dealing with Lars and Tiny and making sure the loops are closed here on Earth."

"Back to work for both of us then," Kaden said, standing.

She rose, refusing to look him in the eye. "Yes. In fact, I might as well get started on those transfer papers. I'll see you at the dock before your departure this evening so that I can have Zim released into your custody."

"Good. Thanks."

He seemed to be stalling, as if he wanted to say something. Probably something lame like an apology for treating her like a slave while she was on Xarta. That she couldn't handle right now. As it was, she was near tears, and didn't want him to see how his dismissal affected her.

"Well, I'm off to do some of that paperwork. I'll see you later, Kaden." She hurried out the door, nearly running toward the ladies' restroom. She hid in a stall and let the tears fall, feeling stupid in so many different ways.

She loved him. That was the foremost stupid thing she had done. She had fallen in love with a man who didn't want her.

* * * * *

Kaden paced the dock of the transport area, looking for Marina. The ship would be taking off as soon as she arrived with the transfer papers for Zim, who was neatly chained for the trip, minus one arm, of course.

If Kaden had his way, he'd be minus one dick, too. But there were limits to what he could do to a prisoner. Legally, anyway.

Spending the rest of his life rotting away in a Xartanian prison would be more than enough justice for Zim. Their prisons weren't nearly as humane as those in other galaxies. Zim would be lucky to survive one year.

The exhaust from the transport blew white smoke throughout the station as it fired up its rockets, preparing for takeoff. Marina appeared through the doorway, strolling sexily along the walkway as she approached.

Even in her crisp, boring uniform, she exuded sexuality, and Kaden felt his cock hardening, remembering all the times she'd touched him, sucked him, made love with him.

She had given herself totally to him in a way that had surprised him.

But none of that mattered now. They'd had an interlude of wonderful sex and shared passions. An affair, they called it on this planet. And now it was over. She had a life she was satisfied with, which didn't include dropping to her knees and sucking his cock whenever he commanded it.

He could tell when he talked to her earlier that what they'd shared had been nothing but a mission for her. Now it was over, and she couldn't wait to get away from him.

How stupid he'd been to think that she'd adapted, accepted and wanted his way of life.

How insane it had been to let himself fall in love with her.

With every fiber of his being, he loved her. Her strength, her beauty, her willingness to please him.

But they weren't a match made to last.

He smiled as she stopped in front of him. There was a dim cast to her normally sparkling green eyes, something he'd never seen before. Perhaps she was still weak from the attack.

"You look like you need some rest," he said, clenching his fists to keep from caressing her face.

"I'll be fine. Don't worry." She handed him the documents releasing Zim to his custody. "You have a safe flight."

This was it. They wouldn't see each other again. He wished…

Oh hell. What was the point in wishing? Without saying a word, he grabbed her around the waist and pulled her toward him, crushing her mouth against his. His tongue dived in and took possession of hers, the last possession he'd take of her. In that kiss he told her exactly how he felt.

Nothing would come of it, but he had to tell her in at least this way.

Before he did something stupid like drag her onto the transport with him, he pulled away and turned on his heel, stepping into the craft. The door closed behind him and he headed to his seat, still tasting Marina on his lips.

Her taste would remain there forever.

* * * * *

The past week had been miserable. Marina thought of nothing but Kaden, remembering the feeling of being in his arms as he'd given her a last, passion-filled kiss before he left Earth. She'd stood there, stunned and unable to move, while she watched his ship take off and disappear.

Her lips still burned where he had touched them, his possession of her as strong now as it had ever been.

What had that kiss meant? She'd pondered it over and over the past week, finally coming to the conclusion that it had been nothing more than a passionate goodbye. They had shared passion. She hadn't imagined that part.

She'd just imagined the part about him wanting to keep her.

She'd never get over him, of that she was certain.

"Why don't you fly to Xarta and tell Kaden how you feel?"

Marina looked up from her desk and shook her head at Laren. "I don't think so."

"Why not?" Laren leaned her hip on the edge of the desk and crossed her arms. "You love him."

She started to object, but it was pointless to deny the obvious. "Yes, I do."

"He loves you too."

Marina arched a brow. "He told you this?"

"No."

"Ah, that's what I thought. You're grasping, Laren. He doesn't love me. If he did, he would have asked me to be with him."

"Maybe he assumed you didn't want to be. Did you give him any indication about how you were feeling?"

"No."

"Why not?"

Giving up on the report she was typing in, Marina pushed her chair back and rubbed her temples. "Why bother? He wants a submissive, Laren. A woman who will bend to his will. While I could do that sexually, I sure as hell couldn't live my life that way. And living on his planet would require it. No, he needs a woman who can give him what fulfills him. That's not me."

Besides, if he'd wanted her, he'd have asked her to stay with him. He didn't. End of story.

"I know how you feel, Marina. And I'm sorry. The one man I thought would love me forever walked away from me and never looked back. I just didn't figure Kaden for the same kind of man."

"Nothing like falling in love with the wrong man, is there?" Marina said, feeling perversely comforted by having Laren to share her pain with. "I'm sorry for you, too."

Laren shrugged. "Like I said. Ancient history. I guess we both just have to move on with our lives and try to forget."

Forget. How would she ever be able to do that?

Later that night, Marina tossed and turned in her bed, her mind refusing to settle into a deep sleep. Visions of Kaden haunted her dreams. His blond hair blowing in the light breeze, the way his gaze raked over her in appreciation for a body she had long ago decided would never be appealing. Yet to him, she was beautiful. With him, she'd felt beautiful.

The piercings were still attached to her nipples and clit, yet they no longer vibrated with life, they no longer connected her to Kaden. Still, she couldn't remove them. They were all she had left of the man she loved.

I miss you, Kaden.

She finally gave up and sat, turning on the light and hoping some reading would lull her into sleep. A scream tore from her lips as a dark shape appeared on the balcony. She reached for her weapon, only to drop it onto the floor as Kaden stepped through the open doors.

Fighting for breath, she held her hand to her heart to calm the racing beat. What was he doing here? "You scared the shit out of me!"

No smile graced his full lips. "Lie down, Marina. And spread your legs."

Despite her irritation, her body responded, her nipples tightening. "What the hell are you doing here?"

"I said lie down on the bed, and spread your legs." He reached for his pants, flipping open the button and drawing the zipper down.

Marina's throat went dry. "Kaden, answer me."

"Have you forgotten your training so quickly? Refer to me as your sire."

"Why?" She refused to ask what her heart hoped.

"I'm here to take what's mine."

Arousal seeped from her slit to moisten her thighs. "I don't understand."

He let the pants slip to the floor, then drew his shirt off, still approaching the bed. "I'm not asking again, Marina. Do it, or I'll punish you."

Still in a state of shock, she couldn't even move. Kaden crawled onto the foot of the bed and whipped the covers to the floor, then drew her legs apart, reaching into his jacket for several strands of silken rope. He tied her wrists to the head posts, then did the same with her ankles to the foot posts. Trussed up and spread-eagled, Marina began to pant in anticipation.

This was her man. Her sire. The man she had wanted to claim her. He was here!

Kaden stood at the side of the bed and looked down on her. "I've missed you, Marina. Spread your legs wider."

Transfixed by his powerful erection, she licked her lips and inhaled a deep breath. Then she did as he commanded. "Why are you here…Sire?"

He grinned. "Normally I'd punish you for speaking without permission, but I find that this one time I cannot. I love when you say that." He sat on the edge of the bed, so close she could feel the heat emanating from his body. But she couldn't touch him.

He touched her, though. Lightly, gently, starting at her cheek and trailing a finger over her jaw and down her neck. She shivered, wanting so much more.

"I'm here because I want you to be mine, in any way that means. Here on Earth, or traveling through the galaxies, it doesn't matter." He leaned in and brushed his lips against hers. Desperate for more, she whimpered.

He ignored her plea, continuing to move his fingers over her skin. "I'm here because I don't ever again want to spend my days without you."

With a quick tug, he shredded the thin T-shirt she'd worn to sleep in. His amber eyes darkened as he spied the emeralds clinging to her nipples.

"You still wear them," he said, awe evident on his face as he drew his finger over first one tip, then the other. For the first time since he'd left, the emeralds hummed to life. He quickly tore the thin panties away and touched the vibrating stone at her clit. "Why haven't you had them removed?"

"They are a part of me now, Sire. Just as you are."

Pausing at her breasts, he circled one areola, then the other. The emeralds thrummed to life again, vibrating against the swollen peaks. He bent and licked her nipples until she cried out in ecstasy.

But she would not speak, would not beg him. She knew her place now, at least in this, and she welcomed the love and attention he gave to her.

Slipping off the bed, he reached for his coat and revealed the anal plug he had used on her in Xarta. His eyes darkened and his lips curled in a mischievous grin.

"Lift."

Raising her hips, she watched intently as he lubricated the probe and slipped it into her anus. She accepted it readily, knowing the pleasure he could give her.

Kaden moved forward, straddling her chest, his cock inches from her hungry mouth. She opened willingly, licking the engorged head, tasting his unique flavor, pulling the shaft inside inch by inch until he began to stroke it between her lips.

"Yes, I missed your sweet mouth on my cock, *zejehr*," he said, groaning when she swirled her tongue around the head.

He pulled his cock away and leaned over, taking her mouth in a kiss that blindsided her with its tenderness. When he broke the kiss, his gaze bore deeply into hers. "I'm here because I love you, Marina."

Her heart stopped beating. Breaking the rules yet again, she asked, "You love me, Sire?"

"Yes. I realized that as soon as I watched you standing alone on the dock when the ship departed Earth. I knew then that as soon as I took care of things on Xarta, I'd come back for you."

"I can't be what you want, Sire," she protested, knowing she loved him, celebrating that he loved her in return. It still wasn't enough.

"Your strength is admirable. Your intelligence, ability to do your job and that feisty nature of yours are only a few of the many things that make you so attractive to me. I don't know where our lives will lead us, Marina. I can't make guarantees. But in many things we are equal. I don't want a slave, I want a mate. A mate with her own brain, using it to form her own opinions. But in our sexual relationship, I will dominate you, command you, and make you do my bidding."

Exactly the way she wanted it. "Yes, Sire."

His cock was enormous, thick and pulsing with life as he knelt between her spread legs.

"Tell me, Marina," he teased, hovering just inside her pulsing slit. "Tell me that you are mine to command, mine to tease, mine to punish, mine to fuck. I want to hear it from you."

He surged forward just a bit, enough that if her legs had been unbound she could have wrapped them around his back and pulled him deep inside her.

But she had no control here. Only the power to give him exactly what he needed. It had taken her a while to understand it all, but she finally had. They both wielded the power and the control, not just Kaden. What she gave to him she gave of her own choosing, which gave her the power. He controlled her pleasure, and yet she controlled his, too.

A very heady realization.

"I am yours, Sire. You may do whatever you wish to me, and I will accept your commands." Not only because it was what Kaden wanted, but because it was what *she* wanted, too.

"You are a part of me. I know exactly who and what you are, Marina. You're a strong, capable warrior, an equal in all things. If I wanted a meek submissive, I'd have chosen a woman on Xarta. What I want is you." He leaned back and dipped his finger along her swollen slit.

The plug within her ass began to expand, warming, filling her anus, enhancing her pleasure.

She whimpered.

"I want the saucy, smartass siren who haunts my dreams. The one who will argue with me at times, if only to receive the delicious punishment I will exact. And always, she will be my sexual slave."

Gladly, willingly. "I love you, Kaden," she said, needing to say his name as she said the words. Perhaps he'd punish her later for not using "Sire". She hoped so.

Her heart soared with the freedom of having told him how she felt. Now, new concerns began to surface. "But how will we—"

He pressed a finger to her lips. "No more speaking. We'll figure out the logistics later. Right now I'm going to fuck you."

True to his word, he thrust inside her. She screamed at the delicious invasion of his huge cock. Her pussy tightened around him and she trembled at the heart-tearing sensation of being one with him again.

The anal plug began to match the rhythm of his driving shaft. It was as if two men fucked her, only both were this man she loved.

His lips met hers, and then no further thought was necessary. Only the simultaneous beats of their racing hearts, their combined groans and sighs as Kaden took them both to the pinnacle and over the edge.

"I want to hear you scream when you come, Marina," he said.

Her gaze met his and she welcomed the tight clenching of her vaginal muscles around his shaft. Her belly warmed, her sex flushed as her orgasm approached.

Kaden was relentless. "Not yet. Don't come."

She bit down on her lip, forcing her body to obey. She wanted, needed this orgasm so badly.

"Don't come."

Oh, God, she couldn't bear it. Kaden murmured soft endearments in his native tongue, words that made no sense to her, and yet she instinctively knew they were words of love.

Still, she held back.

"Now, Marina. Come now, and let me hear your words."

"Yes, Sire! Oh, yes! Fuck me hard, Sire, I'm coming!" She cried out as her climax tore through her, lifting her hips to meet his plunging cock. He groaned and buried his head in her neck, shouting her name as he came hard inside her.

He continued to stroke within her long after their frenzy had subsided. Marina smiled as she felt his cock go softer for a brief moment, then begin to harden again. The anal plug grew within her, pulsing to life the same way his cock was renewing deep in her cunt.

How long he'd keep her tied up like this, she didn't know. But she imagined he had a few more "punishments" in store for her. She smiled, more than willing to give Kaden whatever he demanded.

As far as their future, Kaden was right. They'd figure it out later. Right now, she was his. She would always be his.

He had the power to give her everything she wanted.

And she controlled his heart.

She was his equal in all ways, even in love.

Enjoy this excerpt from

LYCAN'S SURRENDER

© Copyright Jaci Burton, 2004

Her eyes adjusting to the darkness, Starr could make out faint shapes in the room. Why was she in this room, not even chained, instead of their prison? None of this made sense, but she wasn't going to stay here long enough to find the answers.

She'd kill whoever got in her way, but she'd make her way back to Dognelle tonight.

Starr spied a tall vase sitting on a pedestal, and shuffled slowly toward it, her toes sinking into the thick rug in front of the bed. Her fingers closed over the bottom of the vase and she lifted it.

Heavy. Perfect to clout a hulking Raynar over the head.

She froze at the sound of creaking floorboards in the next room. A light shone through the crack in the door. Starr hurried into position next to the door, hoping that whoever came through didn't see her lurking there before she had the chance to split their skull.

The light brightened as the door opened, and she hefted the object, prepared to strike.

Suddenly the vase was pulled from her hands and a pair of strong arms circled her waist, squeezing the breath out of her. The stranger pulled her against his massive chest and she was roughly pulled through the doorway. She squinted in the bright lights, trying to fight off whoever had a death grip around her middle.

"Let go of me, you barbarian! I can't breathe!"

He whipped her around so her back rested against his chest. "Good. Now listen to me," he whispered, his breath warm against her cheek.

"You have nothing to say that I'd be interested in hearing." She leaned as far forward as possible, giving her leverage to kick her foot up to smash against his balls. But he countered by shoving one strong thigh between her legs.

She struggled, and she was by no means physically weak. But her strength was no match for the Raynar warrior. Finally, she gave up, sucking in a huge gulp of air when he relaxed his grip. He turned her around and held on to her shoulders. She glanced up and finally got a good look at the beast who held her.

Only he was no beast. Broad shoulders were centered by a wide chest covered in a dusting of dark hair. His narrow waist and slender hips rested on well-muscled thighs encased in very tight leather breeches. He was so tall she had to tilt her head back to see his face.

Brilliant blue eyes shone from sun-darkened skin. Raven black hair surrounded his face.

By Lal's halos, he was gorgeous.

While she was filthy and smelled like *balon* shit. And why the hell did she care? She never noticed men, didn't care for them, had never had a man and had no intention of lying down with this one.

Clearly, she'd suffered a head injury of sorts. What else would make her react this way to the heathen in front of her?

"Are you quite though ogling me?" he asked, amusement dancing in his wicked smile.

"I never ogle," she said. Not until just now, anyway.

He let go of her arms and walked over to a table against the wall. She eyed him warily while plotting her escape through the double doors on the other side of the room.

"Don't bother," he said nonchalantly, his back still turned to her. "There are guards on the other side of the door."

"Do you read minds?"

"No. You're just obvious."

Bastard.

He turned and approached her, holding out a cup. "Drink this."

"Fuck you."

"Not for a Kingdom's jewels. You stink."

Heat rose from her neck to her cheeks and she was thankful for the dirt covering her face. She couldn't even tell him he smelled just as bad because he'd obviously bathed. "Sorry, I haven't had time to primp in advance of our meeting," was all she could manage.

One corner of his mouth lifted. "Drink this. It's water. The physician said you suffered a head injury and you were to drink water when you woke."

She eyed the glass suspiciously. No way was she going to drink some liquid that could be poison.

Until he took a sip, then held it out to her. She licked her lips, barely able to swallow from the grit scratching her throat. The urge to take the glass from his hands and gulp down its contents was nearly overwhelming, but she'd be damned if she'd accept anything from him. "I don't want any."

He shrugged and set the glass on a table next to them. "Suit yourself."

She was dying for a drink, nearly ready to pass out from the thirst, but she'd never show weakness to this barbarian.

"I've also ordered a bath for you."

He walked toward the door and opened it, whispering something to the guard standing there. While his back was turned she grabbed the glass, gulping the liquid so quickly some of it dribbled down her chin.

A bath. She'd give her right arm for a bath right now. "I don't need a bath."

He closed the door, then walked toward her again, stopping inches away from her. Arching a brow, he sniffed loudly. "Oh, hell yes you do."

Well aware of how she smelled, she crossed her arms, defiantly lifting her chin. "You can't force me to bathe."

His height towered over hers. She'd never considered herself small. But next to this warrior, she felt like a child.

"I can force you to do whatever I want you to, and you will obey."

She sneered at him. "Perhaps you've mistaken me for one of your concubines. I am a free woman, not a slave."

"Not any longer. You are in the Raynar kingdom now, and as a female that puts you under our protection. Whatever freedoms you enjoyed before are gone."

She pushed aside the fear that knifed through her at the thought of her freedom being taken away. "Then run me through now. I'd rather be dead than be a slave to any man."

He tipped her chin with his finger. She refused to pull away, daring him to treat her like one of the many concubines known to exist in this kingdom. "What is your name, woman?" he asked.

"My name is Starr, and I am Queen of Dognelle. You will return me at once to my people."

His eyes widened for a moment, and then he laughed. "You are no queen. No leader of people could be a slight little girl with more dirt than weight on her."

This lower than scum warrior would definitely have to die. And soon. "Bring me before your king. I want to discuss terms of my release."

The tall warrior's eyes narrowed and he crossed his arms, widening his stance. The position made him appear all the more imposing.

"I am Lycan, King of Raynar, and there will be no discussion of your release. You are my captive, my slave, and I'll do whatever I wish with you."

Starr let her eyes drift shut for a second, praying to the gods that this wasn't true. This man, this savage, lived a comfortable life behind his opulent walls while the people of Dognelle went hungry. Ending his life would be her greatest wish.

About the author:

Jaci Burton has been a dreamer and lover of romance her entire life. Consumed with stories of passion, love and happily ever afters, she finally pulled her fantasy characters out of her head and put them on paper. Writing allows her to showcase the rainbow of emotions that result from falling in love.

Jaci lives in Oklahoma with her husband (her fiercest writing critic and sexy inspiration), stepdaughter and three wild and crazy dogs. Her sons are grown and live on opposite coasts and don't bother her nearly as often as she'd like them to. When she isn't writing stories of passion and romance, she can usually be found at the gym, reading a great book, or working on her computer, trying to figure out how she can pull more than twenty-four hours out of a single day.

Jaci welcomes mail from readers. You can write to her c/o Ellora's Cave Publishing at 1337 Commerce Drive, Suite 13, Stow OH 44224.

Also by Jaci:

Why an electronic book?

We live in the Information Age—an exciting time in the history of human civilization in which technology rules supreme and continues to progress in leaps and bounds every minute of every hour of every day. For a multitude of reasons, more and more avid literary fans are opting to purchase e-books instead of paperbacks. The question to those not yet initiated to the world of electronic reading is simply: *why?*

1. *Price.* An electronic title at Ellora's Cave Publishing runs anywhere from 40-75% less than the cover price of the <u>exact same title</u> in paperback format. Why? Cold mathematics. It is less expensive to publish an e-book than it is to publish a paperback, so the savings are passed along to the consumer.

2. *Space.* Running out of room to house your paperback books? That is one worry you will never have with electronic novels. For a low one-time cost, you can purchase a handheld computer designed specifically for e-reading purposes. Many e-readers are larger than the average handheld, giving you plenty of screen room. Better yet, hundreds of titles can be stored within your new library—a single microchip. (Please note that Ellora's Cave does not endorse any specific brands. You can check our website at www.ellorascave.com for customer recommendations we make available to new consumers.)

3. *Mobility.* Because your new library now consists of only a microchip, your entire cache of books can be taken with you wherever you go.

4. *Personal preferences are accounted for.* Are the words you are currently reading too small? Too large? Too...**ANNOYING**? Paperback books cannot be modified according to personal preferences, but e-books can.

5. *Innovation.* The way you read a book is not the only advancement the Information Age has gifted the literary community with. There is also the factor of what you can read. Ellora's Cave Publishing will be introducing a new line of interactive titles that are available in e-book format only.

6. *Instant gratification.* Is it the middle of the night and all the bookstores are closed? Are you tired of waiting days—sometimes weeks—for online and offline bookstores to ship the novels you bought? Ellora's Cave Publishing sells instantaneous downloads 24 hours a day, 7 days a week, 365 days a year. Our e-book delivery system is 100% automated, meaning your order is filled as soon as you pay for it.

Those are a few of the top reasons why electronic novels are displacing paperbacks for many an avid reader. As always, Ellora's Cave Publishing welcomes your questions and comments. We invite you to email us at service@ellorascave.com or write to us directly at: 1337 Commerce Drive, Suite 13, Stow OH 44224.

Discover for yourself why readers can't get enough of the multiple award-winning publisher Ellora's Cave. Whether you prefer e-books or paperbacks, be sure to visit EC on the web at www.ellorascave.com for an erotic reading experience that will leave you breathless.

WWW.ELLORASCAVE.COM

Printed in the United States
77297LV00001B/205-231